This trip was about relaxing in authentic Greek hospitality. No security detail, no flash vehicles, no celebrity fuss.

And it was a good plan...if only her bobbing feet and drumming fingertips would get the message.

Catherine had *tried* to relax on the journey. She'd *tried* to focus on the beauty of Greece, to let the heat of the midday sun warm her, the sea breeze soothe her. She'd tried really hard...and maybe that was the problem. Relaxing didn't come naturally, not to her.

And neither did nerves. She was an award-winning actor, after all; it didn't pay to let her nerves get to her. But this kind of unease was different, uncontainable, and she couldn't deny its source: Alaric de Vere.

Her best friend's older brother. Her friend once, too, many moons ago.

And this was his private island, his place of solace, cut off from the world and civilization, just the way he liked it...

Until now.

Dear Reader,

Love fascinates me. Good thing being a romance author and all. But it truly does.

I fell in love with my husband so swiftly, I would've marched him down the aisle within a month of knowing him and not regretted it. But the thing is, it's not about the looks. Insta-lust based on appearance. It's about that invisible yet intense, unbreakable connection.

The fact that when you're in the same room together, you're impulsively drawn together, as though some invisible force that you can't control is at work. A force that knows better than you what the future holds and keeps that person in your mind long after they've gone. You can have the most good-looking person in the world walk into the room, but if that zing isn't in the air, it's meaningless.

Writing a contemporary beauty and the beast tale, where both characters project a false image, a protective shield that on paper would put them worlds apart, and watching as that underlying connection breaks through it all was so much fun and felt so real, too.

I hope you enjoy it and thank you for sharing your precious time with me!

Rachael xx

Beauty and the Reclusive Millionaire

Rachael Stewart

Recycling programs
for this product may
not exist in your area.

ISBN-13: 978-1-335-40694-1

Beauty and the Reclusive Millionaire

Copyright © 2021 by Rachael Stewart

This edition published by arrangement with Harlequin Books S.A.

For questions and comments about the quality of this book, please contact us at CustomerService@Harlequin.com.

Harlequin Enterprises ULC
22 Adelaide St. West, 41st Floor
Toronto, Ontario M5H 4E3, Canada
www.Harlequin.com

Printed in U.S.A.

Rachael Stewart adores conjuring up stories, from heartwarmingly romantic to wildly erotic. She's been writing since she could put pen to paper—as the stacks of scrawled-on pages in her loft will attest to. A Welsh lass at heart, she now lives in Yorkshire, with her very own hero and three awesome kids—and if she's not tapping out a story, she's wrapped up in one or enjoying the great outdoors. Reach her on Facebook, Twitter (@rach_b52) or at rachaelstewartauthor.com.

Books by Rachael Stewart

Harlequin Romance

Tempted by the Tycoon's Proposal
Surprise Reunion with His Cinderella

Harlequin DARE

Mr. Temptation
Naughty or Nice
Getting Dirty
Losing Control
Unwrapping the Best Man
Our Little Secret
Reawakened

Visit the Author Profile page at Harlequin.com.

For my mum & dad.

For sparking my love of Greece—the food, the people, the stunning islands...

Yamas!

xxx

Praise for
Rachael Stewart

"This is a delightful, moving contemporary romance.... I should warn you that this is the sort of book that once you start you want to keep turning the pages until you've read it. It is an enthralling story to escape into and one that I thoroughly enjoyed reading. I have no hesitation in highly recommending it."

—*Goodreads* on *Tempted by the Tycoon's Proposal*

CHAPTER ONE

'Wow!' Catherine Wilde pushed her sunglasses back, sweeping her fringe away as she squinted against the rays of the sun and took in her home for the next month. A Greek island surrounded by crystal blue waters with a golden cliff face that curved before her and seemed to hug and welcome in one. 'It's incredible.'

'The most beautiful island, *nai*?' Marsel grinned as he lugged one of her many bags off his small sailboat that she'd chosen to hitch a lift on. Her PA had thought she was crazy—*'You know I can sort you a nice speedboat, right?'* but she'd wanted to start this holiday as she meant to go on. Relaxed, laid-back and under no circumstances rushed. So when she'd learned of Marsel's regular trips to the mainland to source supplies she'd jumped at the opportunity to climb aboard.

It had nothing whatsoever to do with delaying her arrival at said island and coming face to face with its owner.

Nothing at all.

She stopped herself from shaking her head emphatically as she threw her focus into the beauty of the island. This trip was about relaxing in authentic Greek hospitality. No security detail, no flash vehicles, no celebrity fuss.

And it was a good plan…if only her bobbing feet and drumming fingertips would get the message.

She'd *tried* to relax on the journey. She'd *tried* to focus on the beauty of Greece, to let the heat of the midday sun warm her, the sea breeze soothe her. She'd tried really hard…and maybe that was the problem. Relaxing didn't come naturally, not to her.

And neither did nerves. She was an award-winning actor after all. It didn't pay to let nerves get the better of her. But this kind of unease was different, uncontainable, and she couldn't deny its source—Alaric de Vere.

Her best friend's older brother. Her friend once too, many moons ago.

And this was his private island, his place of solace, cut off from the world and civilisation, just the way he liked it…

Until now.

Was she truly as welcome as the curving cliff face made out?

Or had his sister, Flo, worked the same persuasive magic over him and left him no choice but to welcome her? A burnt-out celebrity, reeling from a breakup and in desperate need of isolation, if the press were to be believed.

And though they didn't know the half of it, they weren't far wrong…

But she wasn't here just to fix herself, she was

here for him. As a favour to Flo and to appease her own worries too. She was here to do everything she could to help Alaric. To remind him of his life beyond the island, of those who missed him and needed him to return.

Her stomach churned it over, her head thinking the worst, her heart…too tender. Was he really as bad as Flo had made out? The media even? Was she going to make it worse coming here when she was hardly a picture of mental health herself?

'Nai?' Marsel's brows nudged skyward, his brown eyes dancing and bright.

She frowned. *Nai? Yes. Yes, what?*

'The island?' He gestured to it as he leapt back onto the precarious gangplank with another of her bags.

'Nai. Very beautiful.' She gave him an unrestrained smile, thinking only to hide her worries, and immediately regretted it.

His knees seemed to buckle beneath him, his body leaning precariously overboard, and she flung her hand out with a yelp, too far away to reach. She held her breath and was forced to watch as he swiftly regained control and hurried to land, his eyes averted, his tanned cheeks sporting a flush he wouldn't want her to notice.

She wanted to apologise. She knew the affect she had on people, but she'd hoped her and Marsel had moved past that after several hours in one another's company. Her efforts to show him she was just another person, a person capable of carrying her own luggage, capable of laughing over the fact he'd run her suitcase over her foot in his haste to get to it before she could herself, paying off.

But it seemed he was still as star-struck, and after a decade in the film industry, she should be used to it…and she was…

It didn't make it any easier to live with though.

She loved acting. She loved projecting another life on the screen and moving people to tears, to laughter, to joy. To provide the kind of escapism people needed when times were tough or to pass a few pleasant hours of downtime.

But fame came with its pedestal and a lonely one at that.

Not that she was being all woe me. She knew how lucky she was; she just wished at times to be able to blend in, be normal, to have her personal affairs kept just that—personal. Her hand went to her stomach, her fingers idly stroking as the pain of the recent past threatened to invade.

The future would be different; she was determined to make it so. One step at a time. First, a change in career. She wanted to make a difference on the other side of the screen. She wanted to write her own tales for others to perform. Something this trip was supposed to aid with by giving her the space, the freedom and the time to get her first script finished.

Time to work and time to grieve, Flo had said. Time to help Alaric, and time to help herself.

She lowered her gaze to where her fingers stilled over her flat stomach that showed nothing of the slightest baby bump that had once been and swallowed the bubble of pain that threatened to shake her anew. She thought of the soft smile on Flo's lips as her friend had bade her a teary farewell, her own palm resting over her well-pronounced bump. A sight that had brought both pain and happiness, the reminder of what she'd lost contending with her joy for her friend who deserved every bit of happiness.

She pulled her phone from her bag. She'd promised Flo she'd message when she arrived safe and now was as good a time as any. It would also free Marsel to go about his task without another mishap courtesy of her and her world-renowned smile. And though she'd offered to carry her own baggage off the boat, she was relieved he'd insisted on doing it. She really didn't fancy her chances of making it across, bags in hand, not with the way the flimsy gangplank was shifting with the boat. She had to wedge her body against the rail just to text Flo.

She kept it short and sweet, pocketed the phone before she could drop it in the rolling waters and breathed in her surroundings.

It really was beautiful, beautiful and isolated and…quite unexpected. With the simplest of wooden jetties forming a safe path over the rocks, its white painted railing distressed and peeling away, it was hardly luxurious and so unlike the family to which it belonged.

Or more specifically the man…but then what did she know of Alaric after all this time?

The boat lurched with the waves and her stomach took another roll. A roll she knew had nothing to do with the waters beneath her and everything to do with him. She grasped the handrail to steady herself, wishing she could steady her stomach and her nerves just as easy.

She'd known Alaric her entire life. They'd played together as children, hung out together as teens, got drunk and disorderly even… He'd been her first real crush too, in an intensely forbidden best friend's older brother kind of… A ridiculous bubble of laughter cut off her mental spiel—*not helping, Catherine.*

But so much had changed since she last saw him. His entire life had been upended, and here she was waltzing right back into it…surely it was too little, too late?

Was she deluded to even try? To believe Flo when she'd insisted Catherine could help, even when his own family hadn't been able to?

Her phone buzzed in her bag and she lifted it out, glanced at the screen as it buzzed again and again with more messages arriving in quick succession.

You're on the island?

You've seen Alaric?

Is he okay?

Her brows drew together as she tapped in a reply.

Yes. No. Don't know. Calm down, Flo. Xx

Her friend's response was just as quick.

Sorry! Where is he? Xx

Her frown deepened. Good question. Where was her host? Surely it was polite to greet a guest at the dock...especially one that you hadn't seen in for ever?

She typed back.

I don't know. We've just moored up. He's probably at the house.

Three dots appeared to show that Flo was typing...and typing...and still typing.

The hairs on Catherine's nape prickled, her anxiety aggravated with every prolonged second...

She glanced up to see Marsel landside with all the bags, his phone to his ear as he spoke in rapid

Greek. She looked back to her phone, tapped her foot. *Come on, Flo, spit it out…*

Okay. Keep me updated, yeah? Xx

That was it. That was what had taken several minutes to type?

'Way to go in helping me relax, Flo,' she murmured under her breath as she fired off her reply.

Of course. Xx

She shoved her phone back into her bag and lowered her sunglasses, moving before she changed her mind about the whole affair. She needed this break and Alaric needed to get a life, to use Flo's words. It was a win-win.

Marsel saw her approach and quickly cut his call, hurrying to the end of the gangplank to offer out his hand in aid. Gladly she took it, careful to keep her smile to the ground.

'Kyrios de Vere is aware that we are here,' he said once she was safe on land.

'Great.' Though her stomach didn't feel great.

She reached for one of her cases and as Marsel tried to stop her she waved him down.

'I think it will be quicker if I help. It looks like there's a walk ahead?'

She eyed the worn and dusty pier, the sandy pathway through the cliff face, the small cove that looked like it had no decent exit point…it wasn't as though a car was suddenly going to appear. And there were the food supplies Marsel had brought back from the mainland to carry too.

'Is Alaric—Kyrios de Vere—on his way?'

Marsel didn't eye her as he took her other bags in hand and started off down the jetty. 'He says that we should head on up. The jeep isn't too far away.'

'Oh…' She peered into the picturesque distance and saw nothing remotely vehicle-like. She'd just have to take his word for it.

Brows drawing together, she followed him, her mind pondering Alaric's whereabouts. It was perfectly reasonable, she tried to tell herself, that he wouldn't want to greet her at the dock. She didn't have to think the worst. And besides, she was here for her space too, having rejected her security detail and her PA's pleasant company. This was just another element of getting all the space she desired.

Perfectly reasonable. Perfectly fine.

Only…

No one had seen Alaric in a year. The public hadn't seen him in nearly three, and she…well, she hadn't seen him for almost ten…and she *knew* he was suffering. She got that. But did that mean he really didn't want her here, in spite of the invite?

Her heart ached for him, even as the urge to run nipped at her heels.

'Wait here, Miss Wilde!' Marsel called back over his shoulder. 'The jeep is just a few yards away, tucked into a cave out of the sun. I'll bring it to you.'

She blew out a relieved breath, releasing her case with a nod and fisting her hands on her hips. Not that she *couldn't* carry on up the steep incline ahead. She trained daily. She had to. She wasn't one of those actors who depended on body doubles, stunt or otherwise. If the character had to do it, then she had to—it was important to her. Though her agent and the extortionate fee for her insurance told her she was foolish to insist on it.

But a jeep was good. It meant she wouldn't arrive face to face with Alaric for the first time in years feeling exposed and in desperate need of a shower. She'd at least have her trusty armour— her make-up, her clothing and her composure— all in place.

Shielding her eyes with one hand, she took in the sandy cove, the dusty path ahead, the sprouts of green and flora jutting out of the golden cliff face, the trees looming over the edge high above... and then she saw it—a figure...someone in between the trees... *Alaric?*

She went to wave, but the silhouette vanished as swiftly as it had appeared.

Had she imagined it? Was it a trick of the light, of the haze caused by the heat of the sun?

She wiped the sweat from the back of her neck, flapped the front of her vest top to let in some air…

Yes, it had to be the heat playing tricks on her, or it wasn't Alaric, because Alaric would have at least waved.

But then the Alaric she remembered would have bounded down the path and swept her up into a bear hug the second she'd hopped off the boat.

The Alaric she remembered would have made sure she felt welcome.

The Alaric she remembered wouldn't leave her feeling like this…

This was a mistake.

Alaric had known it the second his sister had askcd.

Had known it even as he'd said yes and instructed Dorothea to make up the spare room. For his use, not Catherine's, because Catherine had to have the best his house could offer and that meant his suite.

He cursed, raked a hand through his sweat-slickened hair. Catherine. *Here*. On his island. This was madness.

He'd tried to run off the apprehension, the unease, had ran and ran in the ridiculous heat with no destination in mind, until he'd found himself at the cliff edge and spied Marsel's boat on the horizon.

And then, as the boat had loomed closer, it had been her hair, captivating as it shone like spun gold in the breeze, her presence like a hit of sunshine straight to his frozen core, its warmth far more powerful than the blazing heat of the day.

It had always been this way with Catherine... or was it Kitty now?

Kitty. His fists flexed at his sides. He didn't know her as Kitty, but the world did—Kitty Wilde, Hollywood A-list and idol to millions. Would there be any of Catherine left in the movie star she was now?

And why did he even care?

He shouldn't. Just as he shouldn't have agreed. He clenched his jaw, fighting back the chaos rising within. He'd made his bed so to speak...the time to turn her away was long gone. And he could hardly leave the island himself. Where would he go? Where would he *want* to go?

Nowhere. That was the cold hard truth. His island was more than just his home; it was his sanctuary, his protection from the past, his haven for the future.

But thanks to his sister, he now had a guest, and one he wasn't ready to face, no matter what good manners dictated. He watched as she walked down the jetty, every step bringing her that bit closer, her walk so elegant even as she lugged what had to be a heavily laden suitcase...

He dragged in a breath, battling the sudden

light-headedness. No, he'd wait for nightfall, for the harsh light of day to be gone. In the darkness he could find some protection, something to obscure his scars when she set her infamous blue eyes on him and that picture-perfect smile that had captured the hearts of millions, if not billions.

If she would muster up a smile at all when she saw what he had become...

She glanced up at that precise moment, her eyes behind her shades colliding with his and the world stilled, his heart the only thing capable of movement as it leapt, strong and wild. The most he'd felt in years.

He choked on his own folly as he spun away and broke into a pace that was all the more fierce for the feelings he was trying to outrun. He pounded the trail, through the trees, the landscaped gardens, the burn in his lungs nothing to do with exertion and everything to do with her. He startled Andreas, who was tending to the flowers beside the front door, and almost took out a bustling Dorothea when he burst into the hallway.

'Kyrios de Vere!' She clutched a hand to her chest, her brown eyes wide, wisps of grey hair escaping her bun as she rushed about getting everything perfect for their guest. 'You startled me!'

He came to an abrupt halt, sucked in a breath. 'Marsel will be here shortly. Can you show Catherine around and I'll join her this evening?'

'But don't you—'

'I'm busy.' He was already moving off, heading for the stairs, and he sensed her frown follow him.

'But—'

'No buts, Dorothea. See it done.'

Yes, he was being discourteous, his manners tossed to the wayside in his desire to avoid facing her, but what did they know of it, what did any of them know of it... This was his house, his domain, and he could act however he damn well chose.

He only wished he could dismiss the nagging guilt as easily.

CHAPTER TWO

RIGHT, SO SHE was here, and he wasn't.

Unease rippled through her as she followed Marsel's directions to the kitchen, grocery bags wrapped in her arms. She felt like she shouldn't be here, that she was invading Alaric's home. A man she no longer knew.

All she had to go on was second-hand. Not the hyped-up, titillated news the world's media reported, but the heartfelt version from his sister. And not just the horrific details of the accident three years ago that had taken the life of his best friend, but the mark it had left. How it changed him both inside and out. How he'd cut himself off so completely.

Would he let her in? Would he talk to her? Would he even make himself known or was she going to spend a month alone?

She tightened her hold on the grocery bags as the hollow ache inside resonated out, her own loss compounded by her fear that whatever bond they'd once shared was over. And in that moment, she didn't know who needed it more…her or Alaric.

'Aah, Miss Wilde, it is so good to meet you!' A woman bustled towards her as she entered the kitchen, her brown eyes sparkling with warmth, her flour-dusted cheeks giving off a glow. 'I'm

Dorothea, Kyrios de Vere's housekeeper, and you really shouldn't be carrying those—that is a job for my son!'

Catherine laughed at the woman's flurried greeting. 'It's so good to meet you too, and it's fine. I insisted on helping. Where shall I put them?'

Dorothea hurried across the stone-walled kitchen to the centre island, shoving various ingredients and cooking utensils aside to clear some space on the worn wooden surface. 'Thank you, Miss Wilde.'

'You're welcome.' She placed the bags down and eyed the concrete countertop behind her, its glazed surface covered in flour with a fresh mound of dough at its heart.

'I'm so sorry, Kyrios de Vere's not here.' Dorothea wrung her hands in her apron. 'You see, he is—well, he is rather busy with his work, and—and he did say he was sorry and that he will join you this evening.'

She nodded, though Dorothea's obvious discomfort failed to reassure her and, seeking a distraction, she gestured to the dough. 'What are you making?'

'Fresh pitta to go with souvlaki tonight. It is Kyrios de Vere's favourite.'

Catherine smiled. 'Soon to be mine, I'm sure.'

Fresh baked bread—her weakness. But it was okay, she had a month without a camera on her.

She could afford to eat a little luxury so early on in her break.

'Excellent!' Dorothea's cheeks rounded with her smile as she paused before the Belfast sink to wash her hands and Catherine glanced around the room.

It was a rustic delight, all wood and concrete with a splash of colour from the copper handles and pans, and the herbs that hung along one wall creating a pleasing, natural scent. It was a proper kitchen. Well-used, homely and tasteful.

She couldn't stop her thoughts going back to her host…had he designed this space? Did he cook here too? Or was it all Dorothea and the skill of a talented interior designer?

'Now you should get yourself settled and relaxed.' Dorothea gently shooed her to the door. 'I'll show you to your bedroom.'

'No—no, it's fine. I'll help unload the jeep first.'

'You will not.' The commanding way she said it had Catherine grinning. Not only was she unaccustomed to being bossed about when she wasn't on set, she actually found the older woman's manner quite endearing. 'My son is more than capable, as is his father. You are a guest.'

'Nonsense.' As endearing as it was, Catherine wasn't backing down. 'It's the least I can do for hijacking Marsel's trip to the mainland, and I won't be waited on hand and foot while I'm here.'

'There's no talking her down, Mama.' Marsel

bustled into the kitchen before they could make it to the door, his arms laden with bags as he shook his head and gave his mum a sheepish smile. 'I've already tried several times over.'

'It's true, I insisted.' Catherine rested her hand on Dorothea's shoulder. '*Please*. I want to help.'

'You might as well agree, *agápi mou*.' In came Andreas, Marsel's father, his eyes crinkling at the corners with his grin. 'I've already had the same argument with Miss Wilde outside. She's as stubborn as you!'

That earned a huff out of Dorothea and a laugh from the rest, including Catherine, her nerves readily disappearing in the company of their easy banter.

She followed Marsel back out to the jeep and this time he didn't quibble as he handed her a brown paper bag filled with groceries and took one up for himself. 'That's the last of the food.'

As they headed back inside, she surveyed the grounds once more, this time taking in its beauty rather than trying to spy her elusive host. The house flowed over several storeys built into the hillside, its stone walls blending into the surroundings and giving the impression of a century-old farmhouse rather than the luxury villa she'd been expecting. There were pale blue shutters at every window, terracotta pots with flowers flourishing and well-tended rock gardens with a variety of plants and olive trees offering up some verdant relief to the dry terrain.

The sound of running water came from the lowest tier and she could just make out the edge of an infinity pool that dropped off into the ocean, and rattan-covered seating areas positioned to make the most of the far-reaching view with distant boats and islands appearing as tiny specks on the horizon.

'Stand there much longer and the food will cook itself.'

She spun to face Marsel waiting in the doorway and grimaced. 'Sorry, it really is quite captivating.'

He grinned as he carried on his way and she followed him inside, the cool air of the house an instant relief to the oppressive heat of the day. It wasn't just the soothing temperature either, it was the earthy tones of the décor, the exposed stone and mortar in the walls, the interesting theme of forged cement, wood and rattan flowing both inside and out.

It was calming, Zen-like, and as she breathed it all in, she realised she could be quite happy here. That if any place could teach her to relax, it was this one. So long as her and Alaric were okay…

She wriggled the bag higher up her chest, righted her shoulders and bolstered her resolve. They *would* be okay.

Helping him wasn't negotiable, helping herself on the other hand...well, she was trying.

She walked into the kitchen and straight into the back of a stock-still Marsel.

'Mama! Papa!'

She peeked around him, her frown of confusion lifting as she took in the scene before her— a blushing Dorothea batting away a now flour-covered Andreas. Catherine didn't need to guess at what Marsel had walked in on.

'It's amazing anything gets done here,' their son admonished, shaking his head and dumping the bags on the island.

Andreas pounded his son's back. 'Says you.'

She laughed at their teasing, the speed with which they succeeded in lifting her from her worries such light relief.

She placed her bag down beside Marsel's and brushed off her hands. 'Is there anything else I can help with?'

She eyed the dough and Dorothea hurried over to her. 'Not today. You should get yourself unpacked and settled in.'

'I really don't mind.' Especially when she felt in desperate need of a distraction to fill the hours between now and dinner when she would finally get to see him. Sticking around the family and their pleasantries definitely appealed more than being left to her thoughts.

'But I do.' Dorothea started to shoo her to the

door again. 'Now come, I'll show you to your room.'

'Okay. Okay.' She gave a soft sigh and followed her, pausing briefly to speak to Marsel. 'Thanks again for the lift, I really appreciate it.'

'Yes, Marsel.' The very air seemed to still as all eyes swung to the open doorway and the man now filling it. 'Thank you for bringing Catherine here.'

Alaric!

At least…it had to be…but ten years…the accident and the scar it had left. Her gaze caught on it, the way his bronzed skin pulled together along his cheek, tugging at the corner of his eye and mouth, creating a jagged line in the dark layer of stubble.

Her heart twisted. The sight of the scar in the flesh bringing with it the pain he'd endured, the agony, the loss. It felt like minutes passed when it could only have been seconds, her pulse kick-starting, her eyes blinking away the tears that would have formed as she stepped forward and stalled. He'd said nothing more. Hadn't even moved. No welcome, nothing.

And he was so very different. Taller, broader, the hard cut to his jaw more pronounced as he clenched it tight, his mouth full even in its grim line. His dark hair, neither short nor long, dripped water onto his white T-shirt, the fabric fitting snug to his chest and biceps before gathering at the hips, his loose linen trousers and bare feet far more relaxed than his posture.

Had he been in the shower—is that why he hadn't come to greet her?

It was a nice thought, a relief, but somehow she doubted it, and as she forced her eyes back to his, her thoughts emptied out. It was his eyes that spoke to her the most, those breathtaking blues that conjured up so many memories and seemed to suck the very oxygen from the room. There was no denying who those eyes belonged to. Even devoid of the light, the humour, the love, they were undeniably his, and undeniably cold.

She lifted her chin a fraction and swallowed, her smile so very forced. 'Alaric?'

'Catherine.'

He dipped his head, the movement stilted as his body tightened against the chill spreading within, rapidly taking over the warmth that had assaulted him the second he'd entered the doorway and set eyes on her up close.

She'd twisted her hair up into a knot high on her head since he'd seen her on the jetty, her sunglasses nestled in the golden tresses and unveiling her startling blue eyes that he didn't want to appreciate up close. They made his heart race, his body warm with too many memories, too many feelings. Even when they were filled with the wide-eyed horror they possessed now, her glossy mouth parted, her cheeks flushed pink.

He tried to swallow, tried to regain control, but

everything about her made it impossible. Even the simple hairstyle provoked him, the way it exposed the arch of her neck, her delicate collarbone, escaped tendrils teasing at the skin there. Skin that he'd once admired, tickled, caressed even…only not in the way he'd craved.

And now she was here with far too much of that skin on show. Her vest top hanging from two of the skinniest straps, her animal print shorts lightweight and short. Much too short as they exposed her long legs all glossy and bronzed, and…and he really needed to keep his eyes up.

But then he was looking straight into her wide-eyed gaze, her abject horror freezing over his veins once more. And in a way that was better, far safer. It kept him at a distance, reminded him of how times had changed, how they'd both changed.

'Or is it Kitty now?' He couldn't prevent the bitter edge to his voice, didn't want to, and Dorothea's narrowed gaze told him she'd caught it. Caught it and was warning him to behave. To do better.

'I'll answer to either.' Her smile wavered about her lips, a fresh bloom of colour rising from her chest to her face, highlighting her angled cheekbones and the button-like tip to her upturned nose. Features he remembered all too well and bringing the strangest sense of relief that she hadn't succumbed to the surgeon's knife in her quest to achieve Hollywood perfection.

And why would she change when she's perfect enough already?

His jaw pulsed as he buried the unwelcome thought. 'Catherine, it is.'

'It's good to see you.'

Was it? Or was she just being polite. He hadn't mistaken the horror he'd glimpsed, he was sure, so was it regret he could see now? Regret and... curiosity?

Did she want to see for herself the man he had become? The beast even...

The tabloids were rarely kind, and his sister alone knew enough to condemn him.

Dorothea's brows were wagging on his periphery, telling him to respond appropriately, and he cleared his throat, gave a curt nod. 'I trust you had a good journey?'

There. That was polite. That was thoughtful.

'I did...thank you.' She stepped towards him and he fought the urge to back up, fought even harder as her hands lifted— *God*, was she going to embrace him? Hell, no. He spun away. 'I'll show you around.'

He strode down the hall, not daring to wait, not able to breathe until there was enough distance between them. He had no interest in being all touchy-feely. He didn't want her to see him up close. In the face of her perfection, he felt ever more scarred, ever more damaged.

'Hey, Alaric, slow down.'

He didn't. He raked his fingers through his hair and continued on, hearing the soft pad of her footfall behind him. Even the American twang she'd gained over the years riled his blood. Hollywood may not have forced her under the knife, but ten years of living and breathing that world...was she even recognisable underneath?

Unlikely.

Did he want to find out?

No.

Did he care?

Did *he*?

He couldn't even mentally deny it. Truth was he shouldn't care. Caring led to feelings that he'd long ago denied himself. He didn't deserve to care for another, just as he didn't deserve another's care.

Further reason he should have refused this crazy visit. Refused Flo and not risen to her emotional blackmail.

Flo. His meddling little sister. She'd known what strings to pull, she'd known how to crack his trusty composure—Catherine. She'd been his Achilles heel back then, and no matter how he tried to convince himself that was in the past, that she wasn't his to care for, he hadn't been able to say no.

And what exactly had Flo told Catherine over the years? He knew full well his sister's thoughts on how he lived but just how much of a beast did she think he was? He certainly looked it and Flo herself had tossed the abusive label at him in this very space two years ago when he'd refused to return home to visit their mother after her diagnosis. Called him worse last Christmas when he continued to refuse. But to have those looks of pity, of sadness, from those he loved, those who'd once seen him as strong, successful, invincible... no, he couldn't stomach it.

But then last month, when she'd begged him to take Catherine in, he'd cracked. *'Please, Alaric, she needs to hide away from the media storm brewing before it breaks her.'*

A media storm triggered by Kitty Wilde's high-profile breakup with her co-star and fellow A-lister, Luke Walker. A man who was everything Alaric wasn't and never could be...

He raised a hand to the right. 'The dining room is here.'

He was surprised he didn't choke on the words as he fought a misplaced surge of jealousy and didn't turn as he sensed her pause to look inside the doorway.

'It's nice.'

'It opens onto the veranda and makes the most of the view. I often eat here but you can choose to eat wherever you like.'

He moved off, making sure his point hit home—that he wasn't expecting her to dine with him; in fact, he'd prefer it if she didn't—and he could practically sense Dorothea's disapproving look should she overhear.

'Alaric?'

She was hurrying after him again, but he refused to pause.

'To the left is my study which you won't need. The next door takes you to the gym. It's fully equipped with a treadmill, bike, cross trainer, rowing machine, weights… If you need any help getting to grips with anything let Marsel or Andreas know.'

'Not you? Can't you…'

He gave her a quick look over his shoulder, careful to give his unscarred side. 'I'd prefer it if they helped you.'

'Oh…'

It was soft, filled with disappointment, and the pang in his chest of undeniable guilt almost had him taking it back.

'There's also a steam room, sauna, jacuzzi and outdoor shower.' He was already moving again. 'There are steps down to the pool too.'

He gestured to the right, to the last door. 'The rest of the floor is made up of the library which you can access here. The bookcases are well stocked, so you should find something to interest you. If not, let Dorothea or Andreas know and they will see it sourced.'

'I'm sure that won't be necessary.'

He waited as she peeked inside, her smile lighting up her face. She'd always loved books. It was an interest they'd once shared and the vision of them together on the U-shaped sofa, book in hand, the glass wall before them with the backdrop of the Aegean Sea, was too quick to form. Clear in its imagery, strong in the alien sense of longing it dredged up.

'It's so tranquil.'

He grunted, *actually grunted,* and continued on his way, heading down the stone steps to the mid-level as she hurried to keep up with him. He really was being a jerk. He knew it. Knew it but couldn't stop. Because stopping meant looking at her again. Looking at her and recalling that fleeting imagery and knowing it may be clear, it may be strong, but it was wrong. Because in it, he too was perfect. Unscarred. Happy.

And it made him angry. He could feel it bubbling in the pit of his gut. There was a time he'd dreamed of them being together. Believed it possible even. That one day he'd walk into her world of glitz and glamor and sweep her off her feet. That he'd be good enough. Successful enough.

But the accident had destroyed that dream… not just destroyed it but taken away his ability to want it. Thoughts of his best friend and the wife and child he'd left behind. The guilt of it cutting as deep now as it had the day he'd learned of Fred's death, and he clenched his fists as his fingers shook.

'Wow!'

The exclamation came from Catherine as she

entered the living room behind him and he turned to see her all aglow, her eyes taking in the room, her sigh all breathy and alluring as she walked into the middle and twirled on the spot. 'This is something else.'

He cleared his throat to say something, but all he wanted to admit was that it wasn't the only thing that was. And he wasn't about to let out the obvious. She knew how attractive she was; she courted the cameras day in, day out. Knew how to pose, how best to angle her features...but he found himself lured in by her genuine delight. She had to be accustomed to the best the world had to offer, so why did his home impress her so much.

Unless it was an act?

She did it for a living after all...

'Did you design this space?' Before her eyes could reach him, he headed to the bar at the opposite end of the room.

'Yes.' He took two glasses out from the cupboard beneath the wooden countertop. 'Can I get you a drink?'

'Water would be lovely.'

'Sparkling, still?'

'Sparkling, thank you.' She continued to stroll through the room, her fingers brushing over the furnishings, the neutral-coloured recliners, the distressed wooden sideboard, her eyes lifting to the brightly coloured paintings above. 'I like it.'

Did she like the pictures too? Did she know—

'Did you paint these?'

She turned to look at him and he lowered his gaze, bent to pull a chilled bottle of sparkling water from the under-counter fridge. 'Yes.'

'Recently?'

'No.' It came out gruff. Too gruff. He hadn't painted anything of substance in years. He still didn't have the fine motor skill required in his left hand to do anything close to something he could be satisfied with, let alone hang.

He placed her drink on the side and carried his own to the glass door, sliding it open enough for him to walk out. The instant hit of the midday sun battled with the cool air-conditioned room and he sucked in a deep breath.

He wanted to be able to hold her eye. To hold a conversation. More than anything, he realised, he was at war with himself, because he *wanted* to enjoy her company. All things he would have done—could have done once.

But now, now he felt inadequate, unworthy, broken. Living the life of a hermit with a body that didn't feel like his any more.

He heard her come up behind him and kept his eyes on the ocean, the ripple of the waves, the sailboats all peaceful and serene. 'It was a derelict farmhouse when I bought the island. I had it renovated and extended.'

She walked ahead of him, out to the edge of the balcony, and he followed, comfortable that her eyes were on the view. He paused beside her, keeping his good side facing her.

'I can see why you bought it. I love that you left the stone exposed. It gives the place a soul even as it blends into the land.'

He gave a soft huff, both surprised and pleased that she could see his reasoning so well. 'Part of this floor and the ground floor have been carved out of the cliff. It stops it dominating the landscape and also means the bedrooms on the ground floor tend to stay cool even when the air conditioning is off.'

'You have an upside-down house?'

His lips quirked as a surprising laugh flickered to life. 'I guess it is. And having the pool outside the bedroom is convenient when you like to swim before the day kicks off in earnest.'

'Is that what you do?' She turned to look up at him.

'Yes.'

'Every morning?'

'Yes.'

Her eyes were still on him and he breathed in through his nose, trying to ease the anxiety her continued attention triggered, but it brought with it her scent. Floral and vanilla. Subtly sweet and tempting. He could feel it swirl within his bloodstream, a teasing warmth that he hadn't felt in so long.

It was debilitating to feel such a powerful attraction, unsettling in its gravity, and he reached out for the stone balustrade, gripped it tight. But then he wasn't accustomed to social interaction, social interaction of any sort. He saw Dorothea, Andreas and Marsel. That was it. He hadn't seen another soul in a year, and even then, it had been a visit from his sister that he hadn't even agreed to.

And now here he was, with Catherine. Temptation in its truest form, and it hit him full force once more—his sister had known exactly what she was doing and he'd played straight into her hand.

He was a damn fool.

She turned beside him, resting her elbows on the balustrade and angling her face to the sun, her eyes closed. 'I can see why you moved here.'

She sounded content. Happy. So very different to the chaos raging inside him and he risked a look. He shouldn't have. Ensnared, that was the word for it. Ensnared by the sight of her up close and so at ease.

There was no horror now and he was starting to question whether it had been there in the first place. He couldn't even recall the look as he took her in anew. Her hair shone in varying shades of gold, her thick lashes forming dark crescents over blushing pink cheeks, her lips parted as she breathed out, the hint of tongue glistening between perfect white teeth.

It wasn't *au naturel* though. Her make-up had been expertly applied, the hint of eyeliner following the curve of her lashes, the mascara thickening their lengths, the shimmer across her skin creating what appeared to be a natural flush. Her lips were pink and glossy, as though she had just wet them, when in reality she'd coated them in some expensive product.

She epitomised Hollywood.

And he wanted to hate it. He wanted to use it to keep his distance. To beat back the feelings of old that were threatening to surface and had no place in the now.

'So, the bedrooms, then?' She shifted so quick, her eyes landing on him and narrowing so quickly, he knew she'd witnessed too much.

He cleared his throat, held her eye with more strength than he felt. 'We can get to them this way, or head back inside and go down.'

'I'm easy.'

His pulse spiked, blasted innuendo, and he headed back through the open door, welcoming the chill of the air con that he desperately needed now. He placed his drink on the bar and continued to the stairs.

Was this how it was going to be for the next—how long did he say she could stay? A month? He could hardly think straight and the sooner he got this tour over with the better. His duty as host would be done and he could find some space, some equilibrium, again.

Until dinner at least…

CHAPTER THREE

CATHERINE FOLLOWED IN his wake, an awareness thrumming through her entire body. She wasn't an innocent, she knew desire when it hit her, but this…it had her skin alight, goosebumps prickling in spite of the heat, in spite of his obvious displeasure at her being here too.

And what the hell was that about?

Desiring someone who could barely bring themselves to look at you…

Was it teenage lust coming back to the fore? Was it old feelings trying to find a place in this new arrangement where she couldn't even call herself a friend any more?

A friend would have been able to gain access to the island by now. A friend would have eased him back into the land of the living and not lost the rapport of old. Not that any of his friends, his family even, had succeeded to date.

Was Flo mad to think she could?

'They miss you, you know.'

His shoulders flinched and she paused, her breath catching as she waited for something, anything, but…nothing.

He continued on his way and she knew she'd overstepped already. It was day one of thirty. Waiting at least a week before going in with the whole guilt trip might have been better. Or maybe, not at all?! She wanted to clamp her hand over her mouth, and blamed her emotions that were running high, not to mention the fact that his presence made any coherent thought virtually impossible.

The change in him was so marked. Not just his appearance, but in the way he behaved. He couldn't bring himself to look at her when they were alone and averted his gaze as soon as he spied her looking. He created distance between them at every opportunity.

He was either insecure, or he truly hated having her here, and she didn't want to believe the latter. But Alaric—insecure, shy, nervous. He'd always been sexy, confident, fun. He was the man that had produced the wild splashes of colour on the paintings adorning the walls in the living room. The man who had once made her laugh so hard she'd almost been sick. The man that had stood up at her sixteenth birthday party and sung her a song full of wicked innuendo and tease.

They'd always had that kind of relationship. That unspoken bond. One that they'd been comfortable enough to joke about but never once risked crossing that line. And then life had intervened, her career taking her to LA, his own across Europe. And after the accident…well, no one had been welcome.

She frowned at his back, the obvious tension still pulling at his shoulders. Her chest ached as she considered the man he was now, and the man he'd once been, even as she took in his visual strength. His shoulders that were so broad, his muscles rippling beneath the light fabric of his T-shirt. He'd always been trim and toned. Now he boasted the kind of muscle you'd find in a heavyweight boxing ring, his frame speaking of a strength that would send her mouth dry, if not for the pain she glimpsed too.

She sipped at her drink, needing it to cool and soothe as she watched him turn on the bottom step and point out the first door on their left.

'This is your room.'

He didn't turn his head; instead he pushed open the door and gestured for her to walk around him.

She eyed him, frustrated, demanding his attention—did he really not want to look at her? Or was he so afraid of her looking at him?

She opened her mouth to say something, but what could she say? She was still Catherine, the same Catherine she had always been.

She caved and walked on in, trying to think up her next move, a way to change the dynamic, but the room took over. *This* was her room?

She eyed him, eyed it. Torn between the impressive vista beyond the glass wall and the room itself. It was stunning. Luxury-spa stunning. From the huge bed that seemed to float on air with its fluffy pillows and crisp white linen, the stone walls and earthen floor, set off perfectly by the infinity pool beyond the glass, the thatched cabana and the turquoise sea.

She was accustomed to presidential suites, penthouses, the best accommodation a hotel could offer, but this was his home and all that paled in comparison.

'You approve?' He came up behind her, his close proximity making her back prickle to life, wishing him closer still.

'It's incredible...'

She spun to face him and instantly regretted it as he moved off, pointing to a display panel beside the door.

'You can adjust the temperature here should you need to. Each room has its own thermostatic control. And if you'd rather have breakfast delivered to your room, a quick buzz to Dorothea with the phone beside your bed and she will see it arranged.'

He strode off to the left, through a stone archway, and the lights beyond came on automatically, illuminating what she assumed were wardrobes. 'Your dressing room leads to your private bathroom.'

She followed him, unsure what captivated her more, him, the room or the amazing ocean view that greeted them in every room, the bathroom no exception.

'The glass allows you to see out, but no one can see in.'

She nodded, silent as she took in the freestanding slipper bath positioned to make the most of the view, the double walk-in shower that seemed to be carved out of the rock with its copper dials and oversized rainwater heads, the twin copper sinks that sat like bowls atop a glossed concrete vanity unit.

'There are facecloths, towels, toiletries, everything you should need. The controls for the shower are self-explanatory, but if you need any help, call—'

'Call Dorothea, Andreas or Marsel.' She quipped, rounding on him. 'I've got the message.'

He didn't look at her. Not that she was surprised, and she opted for another approach. 'If this is the guest bedroom, I'd *love* to see what the master suite looks like.'

It was part tease, part vent, and his eyes flicked to her, so very briefly, and then he was striding back into the bedroom and she was hot on his tail, ready to press further until her eyes met with the painting straight ahead. She was held captive by it. The figures entwined, the vibrant colours, the ardent mood, the artistic flick of the brush that she recognised like a signature...

'This is your room, isn't it?'

He didn't respond as he headed to the glass and flipped a switch on the wall beside it. 'You can use this to draw the blinds and slide the doors open, and the controller slotted beside the bed does the same.'

Tentatively, she closed the distance between them, half scared he'd spook again as he re-flicked the switch to stop the blinds that had started to lower.

'I get it, Alaric.' She was referring to the controls, but as she said it, she felt it run far deeper. To him. To what had happened. To how he felt having her here.

He gave a curt nod and moved to go around her, but she reached out to touch his arm. 'Alaric?' She felt the hard heat of muscle flex beneath her fingers, the zip of electricity that ran through her as she wet her lips. 'Stop a second and just look at me…please.'

He eyed her on his periphery but didn't turn.

'This is your room, isn't it?'

'Does it matter?'

'I don't want to come here and kick you out of your space.' *Especially when I know I'm not welcome*, came the unhelpful inner voice.

'You're not.'

'I am.' She wet her lips again, edgy and unsure. 'I don't want that.'

'Believe me, Catherine, the guest room is perfectly adequate for me, and I don't make use of the dressing room as it is. Judging by your luggage, you will…' He gestured to her bags that were piled up beside the entrance, breaking their eye contact as he hastened in their direction, taking away whatever hope she had of getting through to him. 'I believe Marsel has brought everything down but if you are missing anything or you require anything else, just call.'

'Call anyone but you…' She folded her arms across her chest, fought down the rising sadness.

'I have work I need to get on with, Catherine.'

She nodded, knowing full well it wasn't work that was taking him away.

Or maybe it was, and she was being unfair?

'I'll see you at dinner.' He was already out the door. 'We eat at seven.'

We eat at seven. No, *Is that good for you? Would you prefer to eat earlier?* He seemed to give with one hand and take with the other. She opened her mouth to say something but, too late, he was gone. Not even a *Goodbye, enjoy your afternoon*—nothing.

And now she just felt weirdly…discombobulated. A word she couldn't remember ever using, let alone feeling.

The vibration of her phone coming from her handbag proved a grateful distraction and she dipped to pick it up. It was another message from Flo.

Have you seen him now?

Yes—

She stopped typing and bit into her lip. What else could she say? What else *should* she say? Her friend was already worrying enough…

He was here when I got to the house.

How is he?

She swallowed, she couldn't lie to Flo, especially when she was put on the spot.

Different. Distant.

Did you coax out a smile at least?

Had she? No. There'd been the glimmer of one when she'd referred to his house as upside down, but that was it. The rest of the time…

Not quite.

Was he rude? If he was rude, I want to know. I didn't send you there to be mistreated.

'Mistreated?' she blurted out loud, surprised at her friend's dramatic choice of words.

Don't be silly, Flo. It's a huge adjustment for him. You know that. Isn't that why you sent me?

True. I just hoped, with you being you, he'd at least pretend to play nice.

He's playing just fine. Now cut him some slack and leave him to me. Xx

She hoped her confidence would reassure her heavily pregnant friend, who was under strict doctor's orders to rest, and was relieved when Flo's reply finally came in.

Sorry, honey. I know he's in the best hands. If anyone can help him, it's you, Cath. Thank you. X

She smiled. Now all she needed was to have the same faith in herself.

She turned to the glass, took in the pool and the inviting little ripples in its surface...it looked so calm, so appealing.

Yes, a swim, some sun and some time to lose herself in her script before dinner...

Anything to stop her thinking on Alaric and the tricky path that lay ahead.

Alaric couldn't get away fast enough. Being in his bedroom, having her demand his attention, it had been too much. Too tempting to forget how he looked, too easy to succumb to the feelings that should be ancient history and to allow that connection back in.

He headed back upstairs to his study, collecting his drink on the way and contemplating something stronger. Even though he had hours to go before he'd have to face her again, it wasn't enough.

Flo and her blasted interfering ways. This was all her fault.

His phone chimed with an incoming text. He pulled it out of his back pocket and checked the screen. His mouth twitched. Flo.

Did she have some weird telepathic connection going on?

Her message was short but effective.

Play nice. Please!

He grimaced—had Catherine already reported back?

He dragged a hand down his face and blew out a breath. 'You don't ask for much, little sis,' he murmured, typing his reply: I'm trying.

And swiftly put his phone on Do Not Disturb.

It was enough that he had said yes to inviting her. His sister should just be happy and back off. Did she have no idea how hard this was for him?

He shoved open his study door, took one look at the multitude of displays all curved around his desk and changed his mind. There was only one way to rid himself of the tension—the gym. Gym, then work.

Hours later, he'd succeeded in physically avoiding her, but mentally his head had been filled with her. Her smile, her voice, her eyes as they tried to probe, her lips as she'd wet them with unease. An unease that he'd put there, the gesture upping his guilt every time he recalled it.

Because she wasn't Kitty Wilde the movie star when he glimpsed those weaknesses. She wasn't the woman projected on the big screen, in a magazine, on the internet, all confident and untouchable and unaffected by him. She was Catherine, his childhood friend, a girl he'd once have done anything for and a woman so very real and nervous enough to show it.

And that didn't just make her vulnerable, it made him vulnerable too.

He'd spent hours working out, pounding the treadmill, rowing, weight training, cycling... nothing worked. Nothing could shift her from his mind.

By dinner time, he was no better off—his stomach starving through exertion, yet sick with her unavoidable presence.

Play nice, Flo had said.

Did he know how to play nice?

He hadn't always been a social pariah. But then it wasn't the world that had done the casting out, he'd done it all by himself.

Could he at least *pretend* to be comfortable in company again?

For Flo? For Catherine? For the friendship they'd once shared...?

It was temporary after all, a few weeks, and then he could go back to his carefully controlled existence with a sister who owed him rather than berated him.

The peace alone had to be worth it...

CHAPTER FOUR

TWO THINGS STRUCK Catherine at once.

She didn't know what to wear to dinner.

And no mirror existed in Alaric's master suite for her to evaluate her outfits in.

What was a dressing room without mirrors?

Flawed.

She scanned every wall like one would miraculously appear, checked inside the wardrobes, everywhere, and was forced to accept that she wasn't imagining it. There was no mirror. Unless you counted the one above the double vanity unit in the bathroom and there was no way she could check her length in that.

It was all she had though.

Gripping a fluffy white towel around her, she strode up to it and puffed her damp fringe out of her face. She was glowing like a beacon. It didn't matter that the air con was cranked up, and she'd chilled herself off in the shower not ten minutes ago. She could still feel the burn of her run which she'd been forced to do outdoors.

Forced by a sweat-slickened rowing machine, also known as Alaric.

A fresh wave of heat assaulted her as she remembered the view that had greeted her upon opening the gym door. Him, half naked, and rowing as though his life depended on it. His skin glistening with exertion, his muscles flexing with such power. He'd been so far in the zone he hadn't spied her gawping—thank heaven!

She'd done a sharp U-turn and hit the trails that weaved through the olive groves surrounding the house. The heat had been unbearable, but it had beat the thoughts of Alaric that every other activity had let in, her script writing included.

And at least the extra calorie burn would keep the guilt at bay as she enjoyed Dorothea's pitta bread that evening…if only she had a decent mirror to get ready in.

Who didn't have an abundance of mirrors in this day and age? She'd been so caught up in him and the beauty of the house she hadn't picked up on it earlier. But now that she thought about it, she'd seen none. Not even in the gym and all gyms had mirrors to check your form…

She puffed at her fringe once more, eyeing her reflection. She was already running late and the flush to her skin wasn't going to miraculously disappear.

She reached for her make-up bag and froze. No mirrors. No reflection.

Never mind others seeing him, *he* couldn't bear to see himself.

The realisation worked like ice over her skin, dousing the heat as tears pricked. He wasn't just hiding from the world, he was hiding from himself.

She inhaled through her nose, breathed through the chill and the sadness as she bolstered her resolve.

'You don't need to hide, Alaric,' she whispered. 'Not from me, not from you, not from anyone... I'll show you.'

Alaric checked his watch and adjusted the collar of his shirt.

Why he'd even donned a shirt was beyond him. He was in his home, he could wear what he liked, but he had a ridiculous desire not to feel any less than he already did in her presence. Against her notoriety, he didn't just feel ordinary, he felt every one of his scars and more.

Which made him feel even more foolish now as he waited and waited...it was half seven. How was it possible to be half an hour late for dinner when all you had to do was climb two sets of stairs and walk out onto the terrace?

Maybe she too was struggling over what to wear.

Unlikely, but...

He waved Dorothea over as she hovered in the wings. 'Do you want to go and see—'

His question trailed off as he caught sight of movement behind her and his jaw dropped. She hadn't struggled over what to wear, that kind of outfit one didn't struggle over...

Where the devil did she think she was? Some

prestigious awards ceremony being broadcast to the masses? A fancy soirée?

Her hair was once again twisted high on her head, only this time the tendrils that fell were purposefully there, smooth and sleek as they framed her face and brushed against the bare skin of her shoulders. The dress was a daring red, its V neckline dipping low between her breasts and unveiling the curve to each before skimming over her waist and stopping mid-thigh.

She was all confidence and poise, and he was undone.

He could swear his heart had stopped beating, the ability to swallow, to speak, to move from his semi-twisted position, evading him as his head remained angled up at Dorothea, his eyes resting on Kitty—Catherine.

'Ti?' Dorothea pressed, turning to see what had caught his eye and giving a breathless, 'Ah! Miss Wilde!'

She was already hurrying towards her and Catherine smiled, her eyes flitting between them both as she stood in the open doorway, the sunset bathing her in gold.

'I worried you'd flushed yourself down the toilet.' Dorothea was all laughs and smiles, her tease bringing out a chuckle from Catherine herself as she raised a hand to her glossy red lips. Sinfully stunning.

'I'm so sorry I'm late, I—'

'Better late than never.' With some effort he forced himself to stand and ignored the look Dorothea sent him, Catherine's less so. Her eyes flicked to him, her lashes lowering, her fingers fluttering to her updo like it needed any more teasing to stay in place.

'Sorry.' It was quiet, demure, her grimace guilt-filled, and so he felt it too—guilt. Guilt at making her feel bad when it was more directed at himself for not being able to control his reaction to her than it was to do with her tardiness.

He looked away and rounded the table, pulling out her chair before gracing her with a smile that felt as alien as it did awkward.

'Would you like to take a seat?'

The nip she gave her plump red lip was swift and disconcerting. Did she truly feel guilty? Surely she was well accustomed to leaving people waiting—wasn't it just the way of things in the world she dominated?

'I will go and bake those pittas.' Dorothea's declaration broke the heavy silence and, thankfully, Catherine came alive. Less of the cute and demure, and more the composed movie star as she walked towards him, her high heels clipping the stone floor, their beat as pronounced as the uptick in his heart rate.

He clenched his jaw shut, dropped his gaze to the chair as he gripped its back and steeled himself for her arrival. He could feel her watching him, her eyes far too curious. Did she know how much she got to him? After all these years, he should be well versed in dealing with his feelings, especially those sparked by her.

But then he'd spent the last three suppressing any kind of emotion and cutting himself off from the world had made that so much easier. Now he was no longer alone, and he was being tested by the one person he'd never been able to refuse.

'What's the matter, Alaric? You look like you did that day you rescued me from your pool.'

She laughed, the sound and the memory she evoked coaxing out a laugh from so deep within it shook him to the core. As though it were a release, a vent for the choked-up feelings in his chest, in his heart.

Life had been so different back then. *They'd* been different.

She'd been a vibrant wannabe, carefree but innocent too, and deserving of so much. And he'd been a boarding school tcaraway with a chip on his shoulder, angry and frustrated by the constant pressure to succeed.

Was it any wonder he'd been so hooked on her?

'You scared the life out of me that day.' He waited as she lowered herself into the chair, her perfume reaching him and making his eyes close for the briefest moment.

'Well, lucky for me, you were there to be my knight in shining armour.'

She looked up at him and he moved before she could read it all in his face. He dragged in a silent breath and navigated the gap between her chair and his, careful not to brush against her. It was madness. Fourteen years ago, when he'd rescued her from the family pool, he wouldn't have thought twice about the contact. She'd been four years younger than him, sweet sixteen, and the way she'd clung to his neck and looked up at him like he was her true saviour…he'd wanted her to be his. He'd wanted to keep her safe, protected, adored. Before she had become a star, before the accident that had left him scarred inside and out.

But now she was here, on his island, seeking protection from the outside world, and that feeling, the sense of being her saviour, flooded his veins with meaning, with warmth, and he knew the danger of letting it in.

The danger of dreaming again for a future he could no longer have.

He sunk down into his seat, took up the bottle of chilled white from its bed of ice and filled both their glasses. It didn't matter what risk it posed to him; she needed this time. Or at least Flo had convinced him that she did, but looking at her so composed, so perfect before him, he found it hard to believe.

Was she really on the run or had his sister exaggerated the situation to give him no choice but to accept her presence here and to socialise once more?

'Why are you truly here, Catherine?'

Her smile flickered on her lips. 'You know why.'

'Because you want to avoid the press?'

She took the drink he'd poured, fingered the condensation forming on the glass and savoured a drawn-out sip. Was it so hard to think up an answer?

He studied her face, trying to read her; instead he was held captive by the way she pressed her glossy red lips together, her hum of appreciation for the wine teasing at his senses, the way her throat bobbed as she swallowed.

'There's a little bit more to it...' he lifted his eyes to hers, a sense that little was an understatement '...but essentially, yes.'

'More to it?' He didn't release her from his gaze and he saw how her lashes fluttered, a flash of pain that he couldn't miss.

She lowered her hand to her stomach, her eyes too, and he wanted to press further, he wanted answers, but he was also scared she'd break, and seeing her break would in turn break him.

He cleared his throat. 'Flo mentioned that you have a script you're writing?'

'Yes.' Slowly her eyes came back to his, her smile small. 'It's something I've wanted to do for a while.'

'And you're here to get it done?'

'That's the plan.'

'So why can't you do that at home?'

She flinched as he brought the conversation back to the heart of the matter.

'Because home is too distracting.' Her fingers trembled as she reached for her wine glass, provoking his concern, his need to know the truth too. 'I'm sure Flo explained.'

'She explained that the press are hounding you over your breakup with…with what's his name…?' He waved a nonchalant hand through the air.

'Luke.' Her eyes narrowed on him. 'As I'm sure you know.'

His smile lifted to one side. 'Guilty as charged.'

Did she also know he couldn't bring himself to say the guy's name without letting the jealousy take hold? Without pondering exactly what went wrong in their relationship and whether there was some truth to what the tabloids were saying? Flo had suggested it was a load of rubbish, and he didn't want to believe it, but… 'Is it true?'

'Is what true?'

'What the press are saying?'

'Is it ever?' She threw back a larger swig of wine. 'Though some of it is, I guess.'

'So, you did have an affair and call off the engagement?'

She choked on her drink as her eyes shot to his. 'No! No, I didn't have an affair. *Damn it*, Alaric.'

'I'm only repeating what the media are saying.'

'And you should know me better than that.'

'I don't know you at all, Catherine, not any more. That's why I'm asking.' Even as he said it, it didn't feel strictly true. And he'd hurt her in saying it, but he needed those walls in place, he needed to keep that distance between them as he pressed on. 'And, regardless of whether you did or not, wasn't it Oscar Wilde who said that it's better to be talked about, than not at all? Surely that applies ever more so in Hollywood. I'm sure your PR people are working it to their advantage right now, using it to build up the hype before your film launches. You are co-stars with an on-screen relationship after all...'

She cocked her head slightly, curiosity sparking in her eyes. 'You seem to know a lot about my work *and* my dating life?'

He ignored her astute observation and directed her back to his remark. 'So, it's a good thing, is it not?'

She pursed her lips and was quiet for so long he wondered whether she'd refuse to comment.

'I'd rather they didn't...'

'Because you don't like the picture they paint?'

She laughed harshly. 'No, Alaric, of course I don't, would you?'

No, and that's why he was quite happy to hide away. Not that he'd admit it.

She blew out a breath. 'At the end of the day they can do and say what they like. The reasons for our breakup are personal to me and Luke. We understand what—what really happened, and that's all that matters.'

He didn't miss the way her voice faltered. 'Even when the suggestion is that you were unfaithful, that the engagement was his way to stamp out the talk and you left anyway.'

She shrugged. 'It's what the press do. It's the nature of the beast and I'm past caring about the media.'

'Why, Catherine? When we were younger you dreamed of fame, you wanted this, you craved it…in fact, I'm rather surprised you didn't keep the relationship with Luke going purely for publicity's sake.'

Her eyes flared, her cheeks flushing beneath the make-up. 'Do you really think so little of me, Alaric?'

He reached for his wine, burying the stab of guilt as he let the chilled liquid soothe the heat that had formed around his words and contemplated his answer—what he wanted to say versus what he thought she wanted to hear.

'Look, let's not pretend…' The words flowed from him with more assurance than he felt. 'You have a successful career that demands you spend your time in the sun so to speak. You want to tell me now that you wish it all away, that you're tired of it?'

Her frown was more of a scowl. 'Is that so hard to believe?'

'But why? You worked so hard to be a media star, to look the part, to act the part, and it comes with the territory.'

'And don't you think a person has a right to some degree of privacy, regardless?'

'You chose this life, Catherine, you chose to step into your mother's shoes and then some. What did you think would happen? That you would miraculously escape the constant attention she revelled in. Strikes me that you're being all woe is me when you only have yourself to blame.'

She bristled, her shoulders rippling as she shifted position. 'If you think so low of me, why let me come and stay?'

'Because the woman I once knew wouldn't need the sanctity of this place unless it was absolutely necessary.'

'And because Flo asked, you couldn't say no?'

He shrugged. 'That too.'

'Seriously, Alaric, if I thought my presence was as unwelcome as this I wouldn't have come.'

Something jarred him deep inside, his eyes snapping to hers. 'You're not unwelcome.'

Liar.

Or was it the truth?

Underneath it all, was he blaming his sister, blaming Catherine, when really what unsettled him the most was the fact that he *did* want her here. That he wanted that glimpse of life off the island. That, above all, he *wanted* to see her again. Regardless of the fact they belonged in separate worlds. Hers was lit up Hollywood style, constantly in the limelight whether she wanted to be or not. And he wanted to stay in the shadows—he worked hard to stay there.

He'd lowered his guard once and a photo of him had appeared everywhere. The pity, the horror, the open commentary on how the heir to the De Vere empire must feel to have not only lost his best friend, but his famed good looks too.

He clenched his fist, his gut rolling with the memory, the image front-page news…and for Cherie, his late friend's wife, to see him still walking the earth when Fred wasn't able.

'Not unwelcome?' she repeated, dragging him out of his pit of despair. 'You could have fooled me.'

Her eyes burned into his, misreading his reaction so entirely, and a small smile touched his lips as a single thought succeeded in breaking through the pain—she would have come anyway. Welcome or not.

He was sure of it.

She frowned. 'What?'

He gave a small shake of the head.

'What, Alaric? Why are you looking at me like that?'

'Because something tells me that even had I said you weren't welcome, you still would have come…eventually.'

Her carefully styled brows drew together. 'What makes you say that?'

'Because, like me, you can't say no to Flo either.'

Her frown eased into a smile and he chuckled because he liked that he knew that about her. He liked her for being so susceptible to Flo and just as weak to her whims as he was. He liked that it exposed the old Catherine beneath the carefully crafted Kitty Wilde shell.

'My sister is the master of getting what she wants.'

Her smile was full now, her blue eyes softening with affection. 'She is…and she wasn't the only one. You once were too.'

A silence descended, their gazes locked as memories rose to the fore, of good times, bad times and everything in between. The air filled with the sound of insects, the rush of waves, and he wished time away. He wished to be back at that pool rescuing her from her tumble and the torrent of abuse from her mother for being so clumsy, to have her look up at him with the same adoration she had then.

'But I won't lie to you, Alaric. I wanted to see you.' She wet her lips, her eyes alive with her honesty, her…concern? 'I wanted to see where you lived. I wanted to understand why you've cut yourself off from the rest of the world, your family. I wanted to see for myself if—' she sucked in a breath '—if you were okay.'

He was drowning in her gaze, trapped within it, her concern teasing at the very heart of him and tightening up his throat, his chest. 'I'm fine.'

'Are you though?'

He clenched his jaw, dragged his eyes from hers to the sun disappearing behind the sea. The glow casting everything it touched in shades of orange and pink. A small sailboat bobbed in the distance, alone, solitary, and he wished himself upon it. Anywhere but here.

She always saw far too much. She'd always been able to get to him. And wasn't that the true reason Flo had sent her…?

'They *do* miss you, Alaric. We all do.'

He swallowed, his locked jaw aching with the effort to keep it all trapped inside.

'*We?* That's pushing it a bit, don't you think?' Now he looked at her, his derision giving him the confidence to face her off. 'You had no time for us after you made a name for yourself, so forgive me if "we" doesn't ring quite true.'

She visibly flinched, her hand reaching across the table. 'Alaric, you know that's not how it was. You can't mean—'

'Can't I? How many celebrations did you miss

over the years? Celebrations that Flo invited you to, only to find you couldn't make it?'

'I was busy—my schedule was full on for a long time and I couldn't just bail on it, but Flo understood. We always made up for it after.'

He nodded, taking in her words but remaining silent. He wasn't about to point out that *he* didn't see her though, that her claim to have missed him was nonsense.

'Just because I was busy, it doesn't mean I didn't miss her, that I didn't miss you. All of you.'

'No? And yet it's been ten years since I saw you last.'

'I tried to come and see you…after the accident.'

His chest spasmed and he fought back the memories trying to invade, the pain as raw as yesterday.

'But you refused to see me. You refused to see anyone.'

'You soon gave up trying.'

'What choice did I have?'

He gripped the table edge, pushed back from it as he tried to beat it all back. And he knew he was being unfair. He'd been just as busy in the years before the accident, travelling the world with work, rarely in one place for long.

'I'm here now, Alaric,' she said softly, her eyes not releasing him. 'And I want to be here.'

He searched her dizzying blues, seeking a lie,

seeing the truth and needing to deflect. 'Was it worth all the sacrifices you made?'

'What do you mean?'

'To be crowned queen of Hollywood—was it worth cutting yourself off from all those who cared about you?'

'Me, cutting myself off? That's a bit rich coming from you.'

He didn't even flinch as he ignored her gibe, accurate though it was.

'There's nothing wrong with prioritising things in your life,' she blustered.

'No? Even when your mother behaved in the exact same way?'

'Alaric, don't…please don't compare me to her.'

'Why, Catherine? She was the one who told you, day in, day out, to put your career first, don't let anything get in the way—your relationships, your friends, your family.'

'Alaric, please…'

She avoided his eye, but he was too riled to back down.

'Do you remember how it was back then? Why you were always at our house when we were younger? Do you remember the reasons that were given, all variations on the same?'

'You've made your point, Alaric. You can drop it.'

No, he felt too close to something, a realisation, not so much for him, but for her…

'Is that the real reason you turned Luke down?' He could almost feel sorry for the guy now. 'Was he another sacrifice that needed to be made in order for you to remain focused on your dream?'

Her eyes flashed. 'You know, it pays for the press to think and print the worst of me, Alaric. What's your excuse?'

He started, surprised at her direct hit, surprised even more by the strength of his answer that he couldn't admit aloud. It paid for him to think the worst because it protected him, stopped him from falling in deep with the girl he'd once cared for deeply and now could never have.

He wanted to dislike her. He wanted to dislike every perfect inch of her that lived and breathed the superficial world of Hollywood. But he couldn't.

'Tell me what really happened between you both—give me your truth.'

She paled beneath her make-up. 'Do you want to talk about what happened three years ago?'

'No.' It was abrupt, immediate, forced out on impulse. Could she honestly think that whatever had gone on between her and Luke came close to what he'd been through? Had she loved the guy so very much that it was equal to the grief of losing someone? 'I can't see what that has to do with you and Luke. It has no relevance, no...'

His words trailed off as he watched her throat bob, her chin nudging upwards. She was in pain.

She was suffering. But she'd ended it, hadn't she, so why the pain? 'What really happened?'

She shook her head, wet her lips. 'It doesn't matter. What matters is that I'm not all that different to the girl I was ten years ago...' Her anguish was there in her voice, tangled up in a softly spoken plea for him to see her as she was. 'We were friends then. Can't we be friends still?'

'Friends?' It was so gruff, so messed up with the warning siren in his brain, in his heart. 'A lot has happened since then, Catherine.'

'And?'

'Dinner is served!' Dorothea's voice carried across the terrace, saving him from himself and the answer he didn't want to give.

Catherine spun to face her, her eyes like saucers as she took in the heavily laden tray of food. 'Are you expecting more guests, Alaric?'

Dorothea gave a hearty chuckle as she approached and lowered the tray to the table. 'I believe the key to happiness is a pleasantly full stomach.'

Catherine didn't look capable of arguing as she continued to stare at the dishes Dorothea placed on the table, reeling off a description of each. 'Pork souvlaki. Fresh pitta. Tzatziki. Greek salad with kalamata olives, feta, red onion, cucumber, tomatoes, an ample sprinkling of fresh oregano and, of course, a healthy drizzle of olive oil.'

He'd forgotten how hungry he was, but Catherine looked positively panicked and old memories flickered to life, of her eating like a bird beneath the watchful eye of her mother and him sneaking her extra when the dragon wasn't looking…until she'd stopped taking them.

'I should have warned you—' his voice was colder than he intended, the memory making him suspicious of her slender figure now '—Dorothea will see it her mission to feed you up while you're here.'

She looked from him to Dorothea, a smile forming that he couldn't gauge. 'Thank you, Dorothea. This really does look lovely.'

'And it will taste even better, I promise!' She spun away, the empty tray to her chest. 'Make sure she eats, Kyrios de Vere. It won't hurt to add a little meat to those bones. Now enjoy!'

Catherine's smile faltered as she watched her go and he tried to dampen the age-old concern, the anger at her mother and the mark she'd left on her daughter.

'She treats everyone this way,' he assured her while telling himself he was overreacting. 'Don't take it personally.'

But as she turned back to him, her eyes were alive with laughter. 'It's fine. I think she's wonderful!'

He relaxed back into his seat. 'That's one word for it.'

She laughed. 'You love her really… I can tell.'

She unfolded her napkin and placed it over her lap, unaware of how captivated he was by her. Her pleasure bringing her to life and flooding him with a warmth he couldn't contain.

'She certainly has a way with people.'

'She does. It's refreshing to be around someone who says exactly what they think and doesn't try to dress it up for me.'

'Unless it's me doing the talking.'

She gave him a warning glare but her eyes still danced, her lips twitching with continued laughter, and he picked up the basket of bread between them, a peace offering of sorts. 'Pitta?'

'Please.'

He felt himself smile as she took a piece and watched as she lowered her gaze to the dishes spread out between them.

'As much as this looks lovely, Alaric, you'll need to help me. There's no way I can eat anywhere near half of this.'

His smile grew, he knew better. Dorothea's food had a habit of making you come back for more. 'We'll see, you haven't tasted it yet.'

CHAPTER FIVE

'I'M SO FULL!' Catherine groaned, gripping her hips as she leaned back and took in the food still on her plate. She couldn't eat another bite. She seriously regretted that last mouthful as it was, but she'd been unable to resist its mouth-watering goodness. Dorothea truly was an exceptional cook.

Alaric's soft laugh reached her across the table, its husky edge making her very full stomach quiver as she met his gaze.

'Something funny?'

'You, groaning. It doesn't quite fit the perfect princess you project.'

'The princess?' She arched a brow at him.

'That's what I said.' His hand was resting on the table between them and he turned it over, raised it. 'What can I say, it's how I've always seen you.'

Her temper spiked—a *spoilt* princess?! She rose to the taunt, her lips parting to give him what for, but she stopped. There was something else at play in his eyes, in the smile that touched his lips. Something that looked a lot like *affection*... had he had too much wine along with the food?

'Is that so?' She sounded breathless, she felt breathless, which was utterly ridiculous. She didn't get breathless—unless she was working up a sweat the good old-fashioned way. And by that she meant in the gym, on the trails, so why was her mind now conjuring up images of her and Alaric, entangled in the sheets, legs akimbo. No. No. *No.*

She was the queen of composure. But as his gaze fell to her lips, projecting the same heated rush she felt inside, that crown was rapidly slipping. Hell, who was she kidding—it had hit the ground the second she'd stepped foot on his island.

'You were always destined for great things, Catherine.' He relaxed back into his seat, and when his eyes lifted to hers, the heat had gone, replaced by…not quite the cool detachment of that day, but something else. A defeatism, a resignation, and it left her as speechless as the swift heat that had preceded it.

Their pre-dinner talk may have taken a difficult turn. The questionable light he threw over the way she lived her life, her priorities these past ten years stirring up a cocktail of guilt, anger and confusion. The way he'd probed into her recent past, Luke and the—the baby she'd lost. She pressed a hand to her lips, the sudden swell of nausea making her truly wish she hadn't eaten so much.

Not that Alaric knew. No one knew but Flo and Luke.

'Are you okay?' He frowned not missing a beat and she nodded swiftly.

'I really shouldn't have eaten so much.'

She took up her glass of water, praying he'd let it go as he glanced at her plate.

'It's hardly much.'

'It is for me.'

His eyes hardened. 'Is that Hollywood talking, or your mother?'

She took a slow sip from her glass, used it to calm the current within. 'It's me talking.'

He nodded, but his expression didn't ease.

Let it go, Alaric.

Her mother may have instigated her carefully controlled diet, but she was the one who had chosen to continue it. A strict diet and exercise regime were hardly rare in her line of work and she wasn't prepared to battle it out with him.

Especially when it hadn't been the true cause of her discomfort.

She shifted her gaze to the horizon as her hands fell to her stomach, pressing into the tender flesh as she tried to push away the pain and focus on her breathing.

She craved the ease they'd gained through dinner. The smiles, even the laughter they'd managed to share as they'd stuck to safer topics. Like his island, her new movie, her script, Flo…

But they'd just been skirting around the past, his and hers, and she knew there was more he'd wanted to say, more he'd wanted to confront her on when he'd pressed: *'Do you remember how it was back then?'*

Of course she remembered.

How could she forget when she'd been made to feel like the unwanted hanger-on by her own parents? Her mother spending more time away than at home, filming, partying, living the life of a singleton when she wasn't one. And how the De Veres would welcome her in, filling her time with playdates, as her father would take to the bottle, the gambling tables, anything to fill his time until her mother returned. Then the almighty arguments would kick off, after her father had got over his joy at having her mother back, and she would escape once more to the house of De Vere, Anastasia de Vere treating her like one of her own.

'Do you ever wonder how our mothers became friends?' She looked back at him with her question, and he shrugged.

'They grew up together.'

'I know. But when you think back, they never really did anything together? It wasn't like they confided in one another, and when they were together, I don't know... I always got the impression Mum was trying to benefit from your mother's contacts as opposed to...'

'Actually caring?'

She nodded, biting her lip as she saw the relationship for what it was and felt the guilt of it.

'Isn't it obvious? Mum did it for you. She knew how your life was. She wanted to keep you close and that meant keeping your mother close too.'

She felt the invisible warmth of Anastasia wrap around her, so many memories coming forth. 'She stayed friends to protect me...'

'We were all protecting you, Catherine.'

Her heart fluttered with his soft-spoken confession, with the way his blue eyes warmed with the compassion and the affection he'd once had for her.

'Be it Flo with her urgent home study requests; my father when he insisted on yours joining him on some social affair just so you could come and stay; me when I came between you and your mother when she was berating you, sneaking you cake when she wouldn't let you have any, making you laugh when she'd have you cry.'

She shook her head, her eyes welling with the depth of feeling in his voice, the memories he recalled. She knew it all, and yet hearing it from his lips now and wishing things were the same, that he could still look at her like that, that he could still feel for her like that...

'I'm sorry,' she managed eventually.

'Why are you sorry?'

'For being such a burden.'

He scowled. 'You were never a burden, Catherine. We all cared about you. If anyone should be sorry, it's your own damn parents for how they treated you.'

Her throat closed over. He sounded so angry, so vehement on her behalf, so protective. She wanted to reach for him, she wanted to wrap her arms around him, thank him for it all, but she knew he wouldn't welcome it. That for all the progress they were making, they weren't in that place.

She had ten years to make up for—the accident, a bridge to still cross… As for her own truth… once he knew that, he wouldn't want to know her at all.

'How about a walk?'

She started at his sudden suggestion, the surprising normality of it. 'A walk?'

'Yes.' He raked his fingers through his hair, looked out to the ocean glinting in the moonlight. 'It'll help the food go down.'

'Isn't it a bit—' she eyed the start of the trail that weaved through the olive grove '—dark?'

He took in her apprehension with a small smile. 'There are lights that follow the path. I just need to turn them on. I'm sure without the heat of the day, you'll find a tour of the island quite…pleasurable.'

She was surprised to feel her pulse skitter, surprised even more by her own hesitation. What was it about the way he said *pleasurable* that made her blood fire? And why did the idea of going off with him alone feel more intimate than the dinner they'd just shared?

And if it was intimate, why did it bother her so much?

Because your feelings for him are already run-

ning away with you...feelings that you can't afford to let in.

This past year had brought with it enough pain, and this could only lead to more. Her aim was to help him return home, clean and simple.

Anything more...she wasn't in the right place for it. Mentally or physically.

'I've already seen it all.' She took up her wine glass, hiding behind it as he raised his brows at her. She took a sip and smiled to offset the pitch to her voice. 'I took a tour this afternoon.'

'You did? With Marsel? Andreas?'

'No. On my own.' She took another sip of the chilled liquid. 'I went for a run.'

'But it must have been thirty degrees.'

'Thirty-one, not that I'm counting.'

He shook his head. 'Do you often run in hot climates?'

'It's not a favourite pastime of mine, no. But then...'

She stopped as the memory of why she had came back to her, in all its muscular, blazing hot glory. She sipped more wine, praying her pulse would calm, the nervous flutter to her stomach would ease and the heat...she really needed that long gone.

'But then?'

She hummed into her glass.

'You said it wasn't what you wanted to do, but then...?'

Oh, dear...

'When I went to use the gym, you were already in there...' She forced herself to hold his eye, even as her cheeks burned with the admission, and it wasn't the only part of her continuing to warm. 'I got the impression you didn't want to be disturbed.'

His eyes raked over her and she was convinced he could read it all. Where were her acting skills when she really needed them?

'So, you took to the trails?'

'I did.'

'I hope you wore sunscreen.'

She wriggled in her seat. 'If you're referring to the fact that I'm looking a little pink, my skin... it just does that.' It wasn't the fact that the heat of desire currently had her entire insides aflame.

'You should be more careful.'

The severity of his tone jarred her and she frowned. 'Okay, Mum.'

'I'm serious, Catherine. The sun isn't safe, and with your skin tone—'

'I know that, Alaric, I'm not a child.'

He fisted his hand upon the table, his tension palpable. What on earth...?

Anastasia. His mum. The cancer. Oh, God, she was an insensitive idiot. She reached across the table, her hand covering his before she could stop it. 'I'm sorry... I'll be more careful, okay?'

Slowly, he unravelled his fist and, for the briefest of moments, their palms touched. She wanted to keep him there, hold his hand in hers as she addressed the real cause of his concern.

'Anastasia…' She cleared her throat, settling back into her seat as he did the same. 'Flo tells me she's doing okay now.'

'She is.' His eyes glinted back at her, the lines bracketing his mouth cutting deep. 'But cancer's cancer. You live in fear that it'll return.'

'I know.' She chewed the corner of her lip, a second's hesitation as she debated whether to say more and knowing she had to. 'Which is why your refusal to go home is all the more concerning, don't you see?'

'Clever, Catherine. Very clever.'

'What is?'

'Turning this around on me.'

'I wasn't, I was just—' He started to rise and she frowned up at him, her stomach plummeting. 'I thought we were going for a walk.'

'I'm not so sure it's a good idea after all.'

'Seriously, Alaric.' She stood to face him. 'I'm sorry I brought it up but…'

'You promised Flo?'

'Even if I hadn't—' she held his eye, determined '—I would still be asking you the same.'

They stared at one another, locked in a battle of wills. She wasn't ready to call it a night now. She didn't want it to end with him running from her.

'Here's the deal—you keep those thoughts to yourself and we can have our walk.'

She managed the smallest of smiles. 'Or we can run if you like?'

He rewarded her tease with a soft laugh. 'After all that food?'

'Good point.'

But neither of them moved.

An invisible cord seemed to wrap itself around them, urging their bodies closer and closer. Her breaths shortened as his smile evaporated, his eyes falling to her lips that she had unconsciously wet, their depths darkening and full of…want.

He wanted her. Alaric de Vere wanted her.

He wasn't keeping his distance now. He wasn't pushing her away. And then his eyes flickered with some silent thought.

'Though I suggest you change your shoes.'

She swallowed the remnants of lust choking up her throat. 'My shoes?'

'Yes, your shoes.' He pocketed his hands, his mouth a tight line as he looked away. Had she misread the desire there, had it all been in her own head? 'If you've been for a run, you know how rocky the terrain is.'

She glanced down at her impractical heals. 'Of course.'

'And perhaps a jacket? The sea breeze can make it quite chilly at night.'

'Jacket. Shoes. Sure.'

She wanted to cringe. What did she sound like? But then his eyes returned to her, trailing over her front, taking in her exposed skin and the goosebumps now rife, and she forgot her shame. How could a simple look feel like a caress? And why was she craving it so badly?

'Alaric…'

'Yes?'

What would he say, what would he *do*, if he knew the goosebumps had nothing to do with the chill in the air, and everything to do with her body responding to him?

A dangerous question to ponder, Catherine.

She sucked in a breath and forced her legs to move. 'I'll be right back.'

This trip wasn't about reigniting old feelings, it was about the future, his with his family, hers with her work…

And here she was letting her teenage fantasies run away with her as though he was an everyday hot-blooded male and not Alaric. A man who'd been through hell, a man who she wanted to help, not confuse further by…by…

It was selfish, inconsiderate…not happening.

She blew out another breath, trying to let out the pent-up desire with it. She'd barely kept a lid on her feelings for him in her teens. Now she was older, wiser and a world-renowned actor, she should be able to do better.

But saying it and doing it were two different

things and the one thing this trip had already proved—her acting skills were non-existent when he was around.

Alaric focused on clearing the table, ignoring Dorothea's protests that she would do it and the probing stare that followed. She was far too attuned to him and his ways and she knew Catherine had some hold over him. A hold he wasn't willing to succumb to.

'She is even more beautiful in person, I think.'

He grunted his response as he helped her load the dishwasher and cringed as she gave a little chuckle.

'I don't need you to say it's so, I see it in your face.'

'Dorothea, may I remind you I pay you to look after this house and my needs and not—'

She fisted her hands on her hips and stared up at him, the action enough to shut him up as quickly as his own mother would. 'Yes, you do, but I know you, and I think she is good for you. It's about time you brought somebody here.'

'I didn't bring her here, my sister did.'

She smiled at him, her eyes welling up—*oh, God*.

'And your sister knows you even better. You mark my words—this is a turning point for you.'

'There is no turning point for me. Catherine is here to write, and in a month, she'll be gone.'

Dorothea gave a little hum, waving off his severity. 'If you say so, *kyrios*. Now go, I have this in hand.'

He hesitated, needing to convince her he was right. Not that he could. Dorothea would maintain her own counsel regardless, but still it nagged at him.

Or was it more that he needed to convince himself?

Convince himself and delay his return to Catherine because he wasn't ready to face her yet. And it was madness.

He'd cut himself off from the world because he couldn't stand to be in the presence of others, of people who saw his scars and pitied him. Felt sorry for him. Or worse, resented him for surviving the plane crash when Fred hadn't been so lucky. He gulped down the surge of emotion—no, he resented himself enough for that.

But Catherine didn't look at him in any of those ways. That wasn't what he'd witnessed across the table, or when she'd stood before him and looked up into his eyes…

And he'd come so close to succumbing, so close to pulling her into him and kissing those lips that she'd softly parted, subtly wet…

It was the force of that need that had scared the hell out of him.

'Go, *kyrios*!' Dorothea woke him from his stupor, shooing him to the door, her cheeks aglow, her eyes alive. 'Now enjoy your walk.'

She was off her dear sweet mind if she thought he'd let something happen between him and Catherine. Yes, they had a past. Yes, he had feelings for her. But she was a movie star with a life that demanded attention. He, on the other hand, belonged in the shadows and the sooner those around him realised it the better.

Those around you? He could hear the inner voice laughing at him. *You mean you. You're the one getting carried away under her attention, you're the one who wanted to kiss her and forget all else, you're the one losing sight of reality.*

He thrust his fingers through his hair. To even think someone as beautiful and as perfect as Catherine would want him was foolish. To want to act on that thought, foolish still. So why couldn't he shoot it down?

Perhaps because here, on his island, there were no observers, no one to judge a moment's happiness and provoke the survivor's guilt that kept him here.

You don't need others to judge you, you judge yourself enough.

He strode back out onto the terrace far sooner than was wise. He wasn't ready to see her, and yet there she was, a small shawl over her shoulders, the red dress that he'd been unable to take his eyes off and—his lips twitched—white trainers on her

feet. To his mind she'd never looked more beautiful and more endearing to his disobeying heart.

She wasn't his. She would never be his. So why
was his heart beating to a different tune entirely?

'I thought you'd got lost.'

His smile spread. 'In my own home?'

'Crazy, I know. But the thought was there.' She
smiled up at him as he joined her, her arm slipping
through his like it was the most natural thing in
the world. 'So, lead the way…'

He reached into his pocket for his phone, ac-
cessed the app that controlled the lighting for the
entire island and lit the trail.

She clutched him closer with an excited gasp.
'Oh, Alaric, it's stunning!'

Ahead uplighters in the path glowed soft white,
complemented by the fairy lights that weaved
through the trees in the olive grove.

'When you said it was lit, I wasn't expecting
this…since when did you become an old romantic.'

'Romantic?' He gave a choked laugh. 'It has
nothing to do with me, I can assure you.'

'No?' She was looking up at him and he kept
his eyes on the trail, one foot moving in front of
the other. She was too close like this, too comforting, too easy to relax into and forget every worry.

'It's all down to Andreas and Dorothea.'

'Do they live on the island with you?'

'Yes, but Marsel lives back on the mainland. It's far too quiet here to keep him happy.'

'I can believe it. Whereabouts do they live?'

'They have a small house set back from the trail on the other side of the island. You won't have seen it on your run. It's hidden away and gives them privacy from me and vice versa.'

'Sounds perfect.'

They walked in silence a few steps, her gaze taking it all in, and then she said quietly, 'It makes me feel better knowing that you're not alone, alone.'

He scoffed. 'I'm thirty-four, Catherine. I'm quite capable of living alone.'

She opened her mouth to say more and he got there first, taking the conversation back to where it was safe. 'They started small the first Christmas I moved in.'

'Started small?'

'The lights,' he clarified. 'I wasn't interested but Christmas is a big deal here in Greece and it didn't seem fair to let them miss out, so when Dorothea asked...' He shrugged.

'You gave in.' Her voice was as soft as her smile.

'Pretty much. I gave them a budget and have done every year. As the land has matured, the number of adorned trees has grown and, to be honest, taking them down only to put them back up each year feels like more trouble than it's worth.'

'Plus, it's beautiful and you love it really.' She squeezed his arm and he couldn't stop the smile that touched his lips.

'It certainly makes the landscape more interesting at night.'

'Admit it.' She nudged him with her hip. 'It's beautiful…and romantic…'

He felt his lips flicker, felt the warmth creeping through his middle.

'It's okay to appreciate them,' she murmured, her eyes back on the track as they weaved deeper through the olive grove, the sound of the insects increasing around them. 'I promise it won't ruin the cold-hearted hermit you've worked so hard to project the past few years.'

'The what?' He froze, frowning down at her.

But she's not wrong, so why are you so upset?

'You heard me…' She slipped her arm from his. 'Or do you deny that you've been hiding here ever since the accident?'

He stared at her, his teeth grinding. She was the master of switching topics to cause the most effect.

'You don't socialise, you don't see the family. As for friends…when was the last time you saw one?'

His brows drew together as he refused to answer.

'You were the life and soul of the party once, Alaric. And now what? You don't want to be around people? You're happy in your own company, is that what this is? You, happy?'

His teeth continued to grind, his hands forming fists at his sides. 'We agreed to let this go. *You* agreed.'

Her eyes glimmered with something, some emotion he couldn't identify, but he didn't like it. It had his gut twisting, his heart pounding too loud in his ears. 'I did, and I'm sorry.'

He tried to take a steadying breath, but it was filled with her perfume, caught up in the scent of the earth as the sprinklers came alive at ground level, dousing the sun-burned earth.

She reached out, both palms soft on his chest as she nipped her bottom lip in her teeth and gazed up at him, the fairy lights twinkling in her darkened blues and he couldn't look away, couldn't step back.

'I'm sorry to press you, Alaric, I really am. But I'm doing it because people out there…they care about you… *I* care about you.'

His heart squeezed in his chest, his eyes falling to her lips. He only had to bow his head and he could taste them, taste her. How many times had he dreamt of it? Of kissing her, of forking his hands through her golden hair and holding her to him. And now she was pressing closer, or was he moving in?

'Alaric?'

He swallowed past the wedge in his throat.

What was he doing? What were they doing? She smoothed her hands up his chest and he knew he should stop her, but he couldn't make his body obey as it thrived on the human contact, not just anyone's but hers.

'Is this what keeps you away?' She cupped his cheek, her thumb not quite sweeping over the scar tissue there—was she afraid of hurting him?

His heart pulsed. 'Leave it alone, Catherine.' It was a growl, a plea. He gripped her wrist and still he couldn't pull her away. It felt too good be touched, to be caught up in her spell.

'I don't want to leave it alone.'

'I'm perfectly happy here.' His voice shook, his body ached. The years of abstinence, the years of not being around people, and now he had her, hypnotising him with her touch, the look of want in her eyes. But she can't want him. Not now. No one could.

'Are you though?' She raised her other hand, cupped his other cheek. 'Truthfully?'

'What are you doing, Catherine?' He tightened his hold on her wrist, brought his hand up to grip her other, her eyes teasing at him, her lips so close, her scent…

'Kiss me, Alaric.'

Kiss me, Alaric…

His ears burned with her breathy request, need sparking so fierce inside, and he needed to quash it. He needed this under control, he needed her to know this couldn't happen. It would never happen. He didn't deserve the happiness she could so readily bring.

But one taste, just one fleeting moment…to know how her lips felt, to know how she tasted…

'What is it you're so afraid of?'

He didn't answer. He couldn't. And so he did the one thing guaranteed to silence her. He kissed her and lost sight of everything—the accident, the past, the reasons this shouldn't happen—all in the brush of her lips against his, the warm sanctity of her mouth, her whimper…oh, that whimper. It was like heaven to his tortured soul, balm to a wound he never thought he'd see gone.

'Catherine…' It was pained, desperate.

'Yes, Alaric,' she moaned against his mouth, her teeth nipping at his bottom lip, her body curving into him. 'I want you.'

I want you.

Only it wasn't Catherine he heard, it was Kitty Wilde. Those same words to her on-screen lover in a recent movie—yes, he'd watched them all, like some twisted fool who wished to taunt himself with her presence when he knew they could never be. Only…

He opened his eyes, saw *her*, and felt everything he knew to be real shatter.

He shook his head, trying to clear the lustful fog, to separate reality from fantasy. 'We can't do this. It's wrong.'

She stepped toward him and he backed away.

'Why? I know you wanted that kiss as much as I did.'

He couldn't look at her. He wanted it more. He was certain of it. And he didn't deserve to get what he wanted. He didn't. Especially with her.

'It's late, we should get back.'

'We've barely stepped out.'

'It's enough.'

He started back towards the house. He needed space between them. Air to breathe that wasn't filled with her perfume, her temptation.

'Alaric.' She raced up behind him, touched a hand to his shoulder. 'Please!'

He stopped, unable to deny the plea in her voice. 'What?'

'I don't know what's going on here, what's happening between us, but I didn't imagine the way you kissed me back.'

His head dropped forward. He was a selfish fool, an idiot. He hated himself for it. A moment's weakness, a lifetime of guilt—is that how this would go?

'Why are you running away from me?'

'I'm not running away, I'm…'

He was what? She was right. He was running, as far away from the messy feelings she had stirred back to life and the guilt that was swallowing him whole.

'What is it you're so afraid of?'

He spun to face her, uncaring that she was so very close and that the light of the house illuminated every ugly inch of his facial deformity as he used it as a weapon now. A weapon and a defence.

'Look at me, Catherine.' He gripped her arms to hold her close. '*Look* at me!'

'I am looking!' She was just as ferocious, just as angry. 'I still don't see your point.'

He felt her tremble in his hands and released her, sucking in a breath. It wasn't her that trembled, it was him. His entire body quaked. He'd suppressed it for so long, the resentment, the guilt, the anger, and here he was letting it out on her, and she didn't deserve it.

'I'm sorry, Catherine.'

'I don't need you to be sorry. I want you to explain what's going on with you. I want you to stop pushing me away.'

'Just because we were friends once, Catherine—' he recalled her question from earlier, using it to inflict the most damage '—it doesn't mean we can be again.'

Her eyes widened into his, the pain he'd wreaked obvious in their swimming depths, and he reeled away, picking up the pace.

'What the hell happened to you, Alaric? Stop running away and just talk to me!'

'*This* happened, Catherine!' He spun on his heel, flung a hand at his face. 'This!'

Her eyes glistened up at him. 'Is that truly a

reason to push us away? You're hurting and we want—we want to help you. Please let us help you.'

He stared at her, struggling to find the words. 'I'm fine, Catherine,' he forced out eventually. 'Why can't you just accept that?'

'Because you're not. The man I knew would never be happy like this.'

'The man you knew doesn't exist any more.'

'Maybe he doesn't...' She wet her lips. 'You can't go through what you have and remain unchanged, but you can embrace the man you are now and accept it.'

'What?' he scoffed. 'Broken, damaged?'

'No.' She shook her head vehemently. 'That's just it—you're choosing to be those things, you're choosing to let your scars define you, to cut yourself off when all we want is for you to come back.'

'I don't belong out there any more.'

'Of course you do and, deep down, you know it too. You *want* it too. I see it when I look into your eyes, I see it when you talk about Flo, I saw it when you kissed me just now...the longing.'

She was stepping towards him again, her hand reaching up to lightly touch his cheek once more. 'We don't see this, Alaric.'

He swallowed, trying to quash the rising tide within.

'We see *you*.'

'But I don't—not any more.'

He pulled away, thrust his hands through his hair as he made for the house—he had to get the hell away from her.

'You can blame the accident and your scars all you like.' She hurried after him, desperation clear in her voice. 'I know Flo does. But you want to know what I think? I think you're scared to live again.'

He shoved open the front door, praying Dorothea and Andreas had called it a night already as she entered hot on his tail.

'I think you're scared of enjoying life and having the rug pulled out from under you again.'

He clenched his fists, kept on going as he hit the stairs at a pace.

'I won't stand for it, Alaric,' she called after him. 'You need to stop feeling so goddamned sorry for yourself and get out there and live.'

He stilled on the next set of stairs, her words striking through the very heart of him as he turned to stare up at her. 'You think this is about me feeling sorry for myself and fearing what life wants to throw at me next?' He shook his head, his smile cold. 'Fred doesn't get to worry about any of that. He doesn't get to wake up next to his wife each morning and watch his own child grow up. He had so much to lose and I... I had nothing. Yet, I'm the one that survived, not him.'

She pressed a hand to her throat, her mouth

parting but no words emerging, and he was glad of it…he'd heard enough.

'Goodnight, Catherine.'

He turned away, leaving her stood there as he raced down the remaining steps.

'You had your family, Alaric.' Her soft murmur reached him over the blood pounding in his ears. 'You had us.'

Pain ripped through him and he shook his head, refusing to acknowledge that she was right, relieved at the silence that swiftly followed—no footfall, no more incriminating words…he was free to be alone.

Just the way he wanted to be.

So why did it leave him so very cold?

CHAPTER SIX

THREE DAYS LATER, Catherine was staring at her laptop screen having tried and failed to concentrate on her script. She'd managed it for two days, ploughing her restless energy into the words flowing on the page, telling herself it was best to give Alaric some space after all that had happened, all that had been said...

But she couldn't shake it now. The haunted look in his face when he'd spoken of Fred, of his guilt at living when his best friend didn't. Worse still, that he saw Fred's wife and child as a reason to feel unworthy of living. Did he really wish it had been him?

She'd spent the night after their showdown searching up survivor's guilt, trying to understand as much as she could. The various symptoms that were so very similar to PTSD—flashbacks, anger, irritability, feelings of helplessness, disconnection, fear of the world, sleeping difficulties, headaches, social isolation, thoughts of suicide...

Just how many did he suffer?

The list felt endless and she, helpless. How could she begin to understand how he suffered, how could she begin to help him, if he wouldn't talk to her? Wouldn't even be in the same room as her any more?

At first, she'd wondered if the impossible had happened and he'd left the island but one look at Dorothea's flushed cheeks when she'd enquired as to his whereabouts and she'd known he was very much here and very much avoiding her.

Guilt had been her initial response. Guilt that she'd gone too far in her quest to get through to him and had succeeded in hurting him.

She'd been far too quick to spout off and gone in all guns blazing.

But he'd got to her, angered her hot off the back of their kiss that had stirred up so much inside. And yes, she shouldn't have done it, pleaded with him to kiss her, but then she hadn't been able to stop herself. Not when they'd been so close and that look in his eyes had seared the very heart of her. Even now it coaxed her body to life, the persistent restless energy rushing through her veins and leaving the words on her screen an indistinct blur.

She closed the lid of her laptop and swung her feet from the bed. It was time to confront him, and if she had to play on his good manners that had been instilled in him from birth, she would do. She wasn't expecting him to spend all day, every day, with her, but they could at least eat together.

She knocked on his bedroom door—not that she expected him to be there, but it was the closest place to look first.

No answer. She pressed her ear to the door. No sound.

She headed up a floor—the living area was deserted—up another and checked the gym. No sign. In fact, she hadn't caught him in there since that first day either. Was he working out at night just to avoid the possibility of running into her?

Of all the ridiculous, desperate...

She was just about to barge into his study when Dorothea appeared from the kitchen ahead.

'Miss Wilde!'

She smiled at her as she took hold of the door handle. 'Afternoon, Dorothea.'

The woman hurried forward, her eyes widening. 'What are you—?'

'I'm just going to see what's keeping Alaric so busy he can't see fit to dine with me.'

'But I—'

Catherine pushed open the door before Dorothea could stop her, strode in and halted, her mouth falling open.

She hadn't known what she expected, but it wasn't this...this *tech den*?

Huge flat-screen TVs descended from the ceiling, at least ten, fifteen even, forming a curve before a sunken platform with a desk at its heart, and there he was.

'Catherine! What in the name of—?' Alaric thrust his headset off and tossed it to the desk as he stood, the speed of the move sending his plush leather chair spinning.

She stepped closer, her eyes scanning the huge screens and the moving lines, the constant flicker of numbers…

Dorothea hurried in behind her. 'I'm ever so sorry, *kyrios*. I couldn't— I—'

'What she means is I wasn't stopping for anyone.' She gave him a small smile—*my bad*. She hadn't even considered knocking. It wasn't like his bedroom where he may have been naked after all. She swallowed, forcing out that particular image as she swiftly went back to the screens. They were the focal point of the entire room, the rest of it taken up by his desk, a water cooler, a fridge, a glass wall that led off into what looked like a meeting room with another flat-screen TV and enough seating for ten.

The entire space was white, clinical, business-like. There was none of the exposed stone and mortar here, the rugged warmth, the relaxed lines of the beautiful building, and she shivered, wishing for the sun again.

That's when it struck her. There was no daylight either. Outside the sky was blue, the sun was bright, it was glorious. But you'd never know it in here. Not a single window existed. Or if they did, they were hidden by cleverly concealed blinds.

Wishing she was dressed in more layers, she wrapped the flimsy fabric of her kimono closer to her bikini-clad body and folded her arms to keep it there.

'It's okay, Dorothea,' Alaric assured the woman who was now wringing the tea towel in her hands. 'You can go back to whatever it was you were doing.'

'I was prepping dinner.'

'Oh, lovely.' Catherine turned to beam at her, hoping the kind woman would see her apology in her face and not the anxious churn in her gut. She hadn't wanted to upset her by barging in here, but her host had hardly given her a choice. 'Your food is always heavenly. What is it tonight?'

Dorothea smiled, her brown eyes softening but not enough to hide her continued concern. 'Lamb kleftiko, another of Kyrios de Vere's favourites.'

'Even better…' she drawled, turning to eye him. 'I assume that means we will finally be dining together again?'

She pinned him with her overbright smile and sensed Dorothea do the same. Two women staring down the giant of a man before them who looked like he'd been caught in a trap. She watched the little pulse working in his jaw and smiled wider. She liked putting him on edge…she liked it a little too much. But it brought out his character. It made him less robotic and more like the Alaric of their youth.

'Yes.' He didn't look at her as he said it. He was rigid, his back so straight she wondered if he might do himself an injury and how amusing would that be? Okay, not amusing, but it did distract her from dwelling on how incredible he looked. What was it with tall, broad men, with dark hair, a tan to envy and muscles that strained the arms of their tee? Especially when the said tee was white with a V neck that gifted a hint of dark hair and was worn with stonewashed jeans slung low at the hips. He was downright edible and—

And you're supposed to be focusing on dragging him out of his cave, not eating him with your eyes!

'Ah, that is wonderful to hear. Company for Miss Wilde at last!' Dorothea clasped her hands together.

Yes, company at last. At least she wasn't alone in thinking his behaviour rude.

Says you, who just barged into his office...

'Indeed,' she spoke over the inner gibe, her voice saccharine sweet, 'it will be lovely to have a dinner companion again.'

His eyes flickered in her direction, his smile more of a grimace.

'Of course it will,' Dorothea spoke up, 'and as it's especially hot today, I will aim for eight-thirty, time for it to cool off a little more.'

'Great.' He sounded like it was anything but great, and it only made Catherine want to laugh. His eyes darted in her direction again and she wondered if the teeniest hint of her laugh had erupted. But at least he looked alive and vibrant in his anger. It beat haunted and lost and…

She tore her eyes from his. 'I'm really looking forward to it, Dorothea.'

'Well, with that agreed, I will leave you both to it.'

And off she went, light on her feet now. Happy.

As the door closed, Catherine turned back to Alaric, trying and failing to prepare herself for how it felt to be around him again. Alone.

'Anyone ever teach you to knock?' He returned to his desk, his eyes scanning the screens.

'Anyone ever teach you how to look after a guest?'

'Thought we'd already been through this. You're Flo's guest, not mine.'

'This isn't Flo's house—island even.' She kept her voice level, refusing to rise to his dig as she sought to play on the goodness within him. 'It's yours and, as such, you are the host.'

'Lucky me.'

She wanted to laugh. She really did. No one spoke to her in this way, not any more. Since she'd hit it big, people fell over themselves to please her, to pander to her…it didn't matter that she didn't want them to, they did it anyway.

Not Alaric though.

He was giving her zero attention as he hunched over his desk, his fingers making light work of the keyboard as he studied the screens. She wanted to ask what he was doing, she wanted to ask what the screens were showing, she wanted to know it all. But while he was distracted, she was free to study him. To watch his muscles flex as he moved, the scarring to the underside of his left arm catching the light.

She wondered how many more scars his body bore and wished she could trace them with her fingers, reassure him as she did that he deserved to live, that he should let her in, let her help him…

The cool air of the room fluttered past her lips as she inhaled softly, her gaze lifting to his eyes that were narrowed in concentration, the grooves either side of his mouth deep as he pressed his lips together.

Sexy didn't even cut it.

'You just going to stand there and stare, or are you going to tell me what it is you want?'

He didn't look at her as he asked and she didn't answer, unless you counted the teasing murmur of a hum that escaped. It was pleasing enough to know that part of him was still so attuned to her, convincing her all the more that she wasn't alone in feeling the way she did.

She descended the steps into his pit, pausing alongside him and mimicking his stance over the desk.

'So this is where you've been hiding?' she said softly, careful to keep the emotional undercurrent out of her voice. The mix of concern, need and pain. It hurt that he'd been avoiding her, it hurt that he'd dismissed their friendship too.

'Just because we were friends once, Catherine, it doesn't mean we can be again.'

Even now those words echoed around her mind and jabbed at her heart.

'I've not been doing anything of the sort.' He flicked her a look and she caught his eyes dip over her length, the move swift but not swift enough. She had her favourite bikini on, a vibrant rainforest scene across the teeny triangles of fabric, set off perfectly by her sunny kimono. The fire was undeniably there, as was the anger at himself for feeling it. She could read it in every taut muscle, the twitch to his jaw, the way he looked away so quick.

'You could have fooled me…' She let her eyes drift back to the screens. 'What is all this?'

'Work.'

'What kind of work?'

'The kind of work that keeps my father happy and my life free of interference.'

'Are you trading?'

He dropped his head forward. 'Are we really doing this?'

'What?'

'Talking about my work.'

'Why not?'

'Because it's work and it's complicated.'

'Too complicated for me, you mean?' Now she

really was affronted, and she knew her eyes were shooting daggers as she stared at his bowed head.

'No—though, yes—kind of.'

'Because I'm just a pretty face, right? Incapable of more than just repeating the words fed to me and adding a little Kitty Wilde pizzazz?'

He turned his head, a frown forming. 'Are you serious?'

She wished she'd stayed up on the platform now, missing the height advantage as he glimpsed the vulnerability she worked so hard to hide.

'Maybe.' She made it sound light and breezy, like it didn't bother her in the slightest. Yet the script on her laptop downstairs said otherwise. She was determined to change the world's opinion of her and show them she was more than just looks and make pretend.

He straightened, folding his arms across his chest as he continued to frown at her. 'I don't think you're stupid, Catherine, if that's what you're thinking.'

'You don't?' She gave a short laugh. 'You could have fooled me.'

'I didn't mean it like that.'

'Hey, don't trouble yourself over it, I'm fine. You wouldn't be the first man to treat me like a bimbo.'

'I'm not—' his frown deepened '—is that really what you think I'm doing?'

'You're the one who won't even try to explain

this to me.' She gestured to the screens and he surprised her with a real laugh.

'Believe me, that has nothing to do with you! I don't understand the half of it. I can spot an anomaly, something amiss, an opportunity perhaps, but as far as the day-to-day trading goes, I have programs that do it for me. Genius programmers who work for me and write those genius programs.'

She tilted her head, her shoulders easing just a little. 'So, you're like a glorified facilitator?'

His face softened into something of a smile. 'You could say that. And lucky for me, I'm good at it. It keeps my father happy and off my back.'

'Flo told me you head up the investment side of the business.'

'Exactly. It means aside from the odd conference call, I can keep myself to myself, just the way I like it.'

Her shoulders were hunched once more. 'Is that why you're avoiding me? You're keeping yourself to yourself.'

'I wasn't avoiding—'

Her raised brow cut him off and he tried again, 'Look, I think it's for the best if we keep some distance between us.'

She held his eye as she turned and rested her behind on the edge of his desk. 'Why?'

'I explained that perfectly well the other night.' His eyes dipped to her lips, the roughness to his voice and the vague flush of heat in his cheeks mirroring the rising warmth she felt in the pit of her stomach.

'No, you tried to thrust your viewpoint on me. But newsflash, Alaric, I have my own mind. I make my own decisions.'

He shook his head. 'Don't I know it.'

'What's that supposed to mean?'

His eyes creased a little at the corners, their depths turning wistful with his smile. 'You always did, even when we were young. Once you set your mind to something, you were going to do it regardless.'

She smiled, nostalgia adding to the budding warmth, the growing connection, between them. 'No wonder you saw me as a princess...a spoilt one at that.'

'Spoilt. No. I admired you for it. Envied you even.'

'You *envied* me?'

'Yes, I envied you. I envied you your freedom. My parents were always on at me, checking on my grades, pushing me to do better, to quit messing around with my paintings, to quit the partying, the fun.'

'Ha! You did go and get yourself suspended from boarding school on at least two occasions.'

'For the record—' he cracked a grin and it surprised her with both its sincerity and the chaotic flutters it set off deep inside '—neither of those occasions were my fault.'

There was no angling of his face away, no hiding the scars as he continued to grin at her, and she craved more of him like this, the need like a desperate ache inside.

'No—' her grin was just as wide '—of course they weren't.'

'They *weren't*. One was a science experiment gone wrong—'

'The fire in the boys' changing room?' she proposed, remembering that story very well.

'Yes! And the other...' His smile lifted to one side, transporting them back almost two decades as she remembered the exact same look often appearing with a glint of mischief in his eyes. 'Well, I can't be blamed for that one either.'

'Sneaking into the girls' school after hours—yeah, I'm sure that had nothing to do with you.'

Her laugh was soft, shadowed with pain. That one had stung back then, discovering he'd been caught with a girl and wishing it had been her.

But not now. Now, she'd give anything to see that spark back in his eye, to get a hint of the fun-loving guy that didn't take himself—take life—so seriously.

No wonder Flo had been so desperate to get her to come.

Though what Flo hoped she would achieve and what Catherine's own imagination was proposing were two very different things. Because when Alaric eyed her like he had not one minute ago, want as obvious in his eye as it was in her bloodstream, he was closer to the man he'd once been and she was fully prepared to tease out more of that, if it brought him back to the land of the living.

'It was more of a combined effort—Fred was forever leading me astray.'

His smile turned weak, the haunted look creeping back into his eyes. Fred and Alaric had been thick as thieves, Catherine knew that. Right up until the accident that had taken his friend's life and almost killed him too.

She swallowed down the lump in her throat as she straightened and reached out, her hand gentle on his arm. 'You must miss him.'

He pulled away from her, his hands shoved deep inside his pockets.

'I…' He cleared his throat, the thickness to his voice clawing at her heart. 'He was a big part of my life. But Cherie, she was his wife, and his little girl…to see me return and not him… It had been my idea to go on that lads' weekend. He wouldn't have been on the private jet if not for me.'

He shook his head, unable to continue, and she forced herself to hold still, to give him physical space.

'It wasn't your fault, Alaric. It was an accident. It could have happened to—.'

'To anyone!' he threw at her. 'I've heard it all, Catherine. Nothing you say can make it any better.

Every night, I go to bed and see Cherie—Cherie and his daughter stood at his graveside, their lives ruined, and mine—mine—'

He stalked away and she watched him, his pain so palpable she could feel it tearing through her.

'How is Cherie?'

'I don't know.' His voice choked. Guilt. Pain. His shoulders shuddering with it all. 'I haven't spoken to her, not since the funeral.'

'But it was an accident, Alaric,' she tried again, softer. 'There was nothing you could have done.'

He angled his face towards her. 'I should never have suggested the trip.'

'But you did, and it's done, and nothing can change that it happened.'

He scoffed and she could taste the bitterness, the resentment, in him. 'Life goes on regardless.'

She nodded, hearing his words, understanding what he meant, but at the same time…

'Your life needs to go on too, Alaric.'

'That's what I just said.'

'No, you said life goes on regardless…you mean around you. Not for you.'

He shook his head. 'Same difference.'

'No. It's not.'

'Don't stand there and tell me I owe it to him to live my life, Catherine.' He spun to face her. 'I've heard it all, from my mother, my father, Flo, my bleeding counsellor. It's not that simple.'

'I didn't say it was simple, it could never be

simple, but have you tried speaking to Cherie, talking to her about how you feel?'

'And put her through that? Put that on her? How selfish do you think I am?'

'You're not selfish, Alaric, you're in pain and until you face it and move on you will always suffer.'

He stared at her, long and hard, but she wanted to show him she wasn't going anywhere, and she wasn't backing down from this.

'It's been three years, Alaric. You can't hide here for ever. Your family miss you. Flo misses you. She's—she's *pregnant*, for heaven's sake.' Her voice quavered, her hand clutching her abdomen in an impulsive gesture as it brought with it the reminder of her own loss. 'Are you really going to miss out on meeting your niece or nephew, spending time with them?'

'Why do you even care so much?' he lashed out. 'You've been so busy the last ten years, pursuing your career, why come back now and interfere? Why pretend you give a damn?'

Her eyes stung, her chest ached, but she refused to let the hurtful words he threw at her in his desperation deter her from pushing further. 'What did your family do to you that was so bad you'd rather hide out here?'

His laugh was harsh. 'Aside from my parents trying to control my every move.'

'Now you're just being melodramatic.'

'*I'm* the dramatic one. Kitty Wilde is stood in my study telling me *I'm* over dramatic.'

She ignored the jibe. 'This isn't a joke, Alaric.'

'I didn't say it was.'

'Then tell me what they did that was so awful for you to turn your back on them, because the way I see it, you survived the crash, but they lost you anyway.'

Alaric stared at her, tormented by the truth of her words.

'What I would have given—' she continued so very quiet, and he wanted to cover his ears like a child as he feared what was coming '—to have a smidgen of the care and attention your parents bestowed on you growing up.'

He felt her pain spear him, his hand reaching out on autopilot, reaching for the vulnerable girl she'd once been and the woman she was now. Neither having had the option of returning to a loving family, and as she backed away, he wanted to howl at the world for its cruelty, its unfairness...

'No!' She held her palm out to ward him off. 'Don't you go softening now because you feel sorry for me. That freedom you envied, I got because my father was too distracted by my mother's absence to care what I was up to. I could have flunked every subject and I don't think they would have noticed. Run away even. But you...

you had parents that cared, a sister too…you still have them.'

He folded his arms, hardening himself to her words as he acknowledged her clever orchestration of the entire conversation. Well, no more.

'And after all your family did to you, you still followed in your mother's footsteps. Of all the paths to take, Catherine, I'd hoped you'd do better.'

'I am *better*.'

'Are you?' He felt sick saying it, challenging her when he knew it was deflection, but…

'Just because I became an actor, it doesn't mean—it doesn't mean…' She broke off, her eyes glistening anew as she clutched her abdomen tighter, and he frowned over the move. Her reaction so much stronger than he could have predicted.

She'd been so fierce, so unbreakable, seconds before.

'My mother and I are nothing alike,' she whispered, broken, distraught, and any attempt to deny it died on his lips. 'For one, I don't have a family to let down. There's just me and my career. No competition. No one to neglect.'

'No one to care for?'

She stared at him.

'That's what you mean, isn't it?' he probed, a light-bulb moment leaving him feeling oddly bereft. 'Is that why you broke it off with Luke? He was getting too close and you didn't want to risk him becoming a distraction or someone you could let down?'

'Don't presume to understand what happened between me and Luke. You don't get to pass judgement on something you know nothing about.'

'I can read between the lines well enough.' He felt energised by the realisation, his defensive walls rebuilding as he realised that whatever existed between him and Catherine, whatever the connection, there was no future.

And it wasn't because of how messed up he was. No, it was because Kitty Wilde would never have room in her life for another.

'You may not have had an affair, Catherine, but I can easily imagine that Luke got too serious, and you ran. My guess is you were scared of becoming your mother, scared of having your priorities skewed, scared of abandoning—'

'Stop it, Alaric. Just stop it!' Her entire body trembled, a tear rolling down one cheek and torturing him with its journey. Had her breakup hurt her so very much? Had she loved Luke *that* much and still loved her job more?

He shook his head, shock stealing the breath from his lungs as his jealousy of the man was obliterated with pity.

'Tell me something?' he breathed. 'Is it really worth it?'

'What?'

'Your career, your fame?'

She frowned, swiping the tear away with the back of her hand. 'You don't know what you're talking about.'

'I know that you're alone, that for all you dig at me for living here alone, you're as bad. In fact, for you, it must be worse. Surrounded by people day in, day out, and standing alone…'

'And I repeat, you don't know what you're talking about.'

'No? Tell me, then, do you ever get lonely?'

'Asks the man who lives on his own bleeding island!'

'And I'm happy that way. You're not. You're stood there crying over a man that you chose to leave.'

Her breath shuddered out of her. 'You don't understand.'

'Then explain it to me, make me understand.'

She shook her head. 'I can't.'

'Why?'

'Because—just because.' She wrapped her arms tight around her middle.

'Then let's agree to leave each other's lives alone. You don't want to speak about Luke and what went wrong. And I sure as hell don't want to talk about my reasons for being here.'

'But, Alaric—'

'But nothing, Catherine, you keep your nose

out of my business and I'll do the same in return. Now I have work to be getting on with.'

She stared at him, quiet for a moment, and he felt a sickening thud in the pit of his stomach. Had he gone too far? Would she bail on dinner? Would she pack up and leave entirely?

She wet her lips, sucked in a breath through her nose.

'I'll leave you to it.'

She started to walk away, and he called out. 'I'll see you at dinner?'

It was definitely more of a question and she stilled, looked over her shoulder, a second's hesitation and then the smallest of nods.

'Good.' His shoulders eased, his breath leaving him as he watched her go. Taking all the warmth, all the light, with her.

He looked back to the screens and saw nothing but the pain in her eyes, the tears, the sorrow…all over a man she had chosen to leave. A man who had at least managed to earn a place in her heart, and still it hadn't been enough for her to put him first.

Goosebumps spread across his skin, a chill shocking him to the core. This wasn't jealousy, or anger, or guilt, this was fear. Fear of how he felt towards her…how he could feel if he let himself get caught up in her again.

Had that been his sister's plan? Throw temptation in his face and use it to lure him out?

Had his cunning little sister been aware of his feelings towards her friend all along and never let on?

And if that was the case, how would she feel to learn that no matter how he felt, or how much Catherine may feel for him in return, she would always put her career first? That, ultimately, she'd break his heart if he let her…

All good reason to maintain his distance…instead they were having dinner together that evening.

And he shouldn't be looking forward to it.

But this was Catherine, and his heart was overriding his head.

'We care… We don't see this… We see you.'

He ran a hand over his scarred cheek as her words chipped away at his defences.

Not once had she intentionally made him self-conscious. No, he'd been the one seeking to hide it, to not let her see him in all his ugly glory, fearing her pity, her repulsion even. And instead she'd given him her warmth, her attention, her kiss. And that kiss… *Wow*, that kiss. A moment of madness, of weakness, that had left him feeling starved and desperate. He couldn't stop reliving it, over and over.

And in the face of such temptation, such acceptance, he wasn't sure how long he could play dumb to the attraction, especially now he was done hiding from her, physically at least.

CHAPTER SEVEN

CATHERINE WAS PLAYING with fire, but she was angry.

Angry at the way he'd thrown her mother at her, angry at the way life had construed to ruin his and stopped for her the second her baby had been taken from her.

She didn't know how dinner was going to play out, but she'd sure as hell made sure she felt invincible. Flawless make-up, glossy skin and a dress to die for. She wasn't going to let Alaric break her again.

If he didn't want to talk about the past, then fine, she'd let it go. On the proviso that he let hers go too.

She couldn't bear thinking on it, let alone talk of it. The pain, the guilt, the shared suffering with Luke over a baby…a baby they hadn't—*she* hadn't wanted, hadn't planned and miscarried mere weeks after the test result.

But in those weeks so much had changed. She had swung from panic, from fear, from wishing it away to feeling a new life growing inside her, of feeling its importance, its unparalleled importance. Her vision for the future changing so completely because she wouldn't be her mother, she wouldn't…

And just when all had felt good again, better even, it had been snatched away.

The ultimate punishment for her selfishness.

Her hand went to her stomach as she froze on the stairs, her other hand clutching at the handrail to fend off the fresh wave of grief, of remorse.

She wasn't her mother. She *wasn't*.

Yet she'd failed her child before they'd even been born.

She sucked in a breath and let it out slow. Not even Flo knew the whole truth. The fact she refused to believe it at first, then the resentment…

How could she even begin to tell Alaric that when he already had such a twisted view of who she was?

No, putting words to it would only confirm what he already suspected.

What he already suspected and what she feared.

That she was as bad, if not worse, than her mother ever was.

No. She wanted to forget and she owed him the same consideration over his past too. No matter what Flo had asked of her, what she had set out to achieve in coming here, she needed to respect his decision.

Taking another breath, she combed her fingers through her hair and shook out the waves she had carefully crafted as she'd opted to leave it down, free of restraint as she wished to be free of the past.

Tonight at least…

He was already on the terrace when she got there, a drink in hand, his eyes on the view. She came up behind him, surprised when he didn't detect her approach, and she cleared her throat. 'It's a beautiful evening.'

And it was—the sun casting its soft glow as it sunk into the sea, the heat of the day leaving a subtle warmth in the air—but it wasn't the reason she'd said it. She'd sensed his thoughts were as preoccupied as her own had been and she wanted him to relax, just as she was determined to do so. She wanted him to know that she'd put their impassioned talk behind her and hoped that he could too.

'It is.' He pushed up out of his seat, his eyes raking over her, and the appreciation she spied lit her up inside.

She did love this dress. How the slinky fabric caught the light and gave the appearance of liquid gold. The slender shoestring straps and wrap style creating a low V neckline and allowing the floor-length skirt to part as she walked, revealing her leg from the thigh all the way down to her heels.

She felt sexy. She looked sexy. And that was the confidence she needed to get through the evening.

'You look—' he cleared his throat, stepped out from the table to greet her '—like you're missing a red carpet.'

Her smile faltered before she could stop it. She was too damned sensitive to his opinion, anyone else and she wouldn't care. 'Too much?'

'No.' The smallest of lines appeared between his brows, and his voice was gruff as he pocketed his hands. 'Not at all.'

'Good.' Her smile relaxed with her returning confidence. 'I have to say you look red-carpet worthy yourself.'

He wore dark trousers and a navy shirt unbuttoned at the collar, the fit emphasising his muscular build and trim waist, the colour setting off his tan and the blue of his eyes. He'd combed some product through his hair, taming the wild strands so that they were clear of his face. He'd shaved too, exposing his scar so completely and making something within her pulse. He wasn't hiding it from her, not any more.

She wet her suddenly dry lips and paused before him, pressing her palms into his chest before she could lose her nerve. His body contracted beneath her touch, his lips parting with obvious surprise as she lifted up on tiptoes to press a kiss to his cheek. It was how she would have greeted any man in her acquaintance, but the simple contact thrilled her to the core.

She paused—a second to appreciate his scent, another his warmth—and then she dropped back, moving away as his arm locked around her, keeping her close.

She looked up at him in question.

'You like playing with fire, don't you?'

Her own words came back to her, her make-up,

her outfit, a confidence booster as she admitted, 'Only when it's fun.'

'Fun for who? You?'

'For the both of us.'

His eyes glittered, the pulse in his jaw twitched, and she pulled away before she could succumb to the urge burning through her very veins, because all she wanted to do was kiss him. Kiss him and forget everything.

One step free, two, and suddenly she was crushed up against hot, hard muscle, a frisson of excitement rushing south.

'Is this just some game to you, Catherine?'

'If it's a game where we both come away satisfied—' her voice was all breathy with lust '—I'm all for it.'

He growled low in his chest, the rumble filtering through to her. 'What do you want from me?'

'Right this second...you're a clever man, I'll let you work it out.'

His eyes darkened above her, his head drew closer, his voice gruffer still. 'What if I need you to spell it out?'

Her lips curved into a smile, power rushing her veins as she reached closer, the tips of her toes pressing into the ground, her palms smoothing over his shoulders and relishing the strength beneath, the hard muscle she so desperately wanted to explore...

She brushed her lips against his, a little flick of

the tip of her tongue against his mouth, and her eyes connected with his. *What are you doing?* came the mental warning, but what left her lips was a simple, 'Enough?'

He lifted his hand, forking it through her hair. 'With you, I don't think it can ever be enough.'

And before she could overthink his words, he was kissing her, kissing her so deep and so thoroughly she was consumed by it. The carnal heat coursing through her as she savoured the taste of his mouth, the pressure of his lips, his tongue as it grazed against hers.

She moaned with the heady rush, her desperation, her frustration…it was everything and not enough at once. She raised her hands to his hair and tugged him closer, pressed her entirety against him. She could feel his heart pounding into her, or was it her heart pounding into him? She didn't know where he ended, and she began, and if they could just stay like this for longer, for ever…

A startled gasp filled the air and they froze, their heads snapping to the left, to a startled Dorothea, who looked about to flee.

'I'll come back!'

'No, no, it's fine.' His broken voice rasped along Catherine's spine and the world seemed to spin. Lack of oxygen through kissing was a real thing. Who knew!

She took a steadying breath, stepped away from him. She could feel her cheeks burning with it all—lustful heat, bashfulness and something that ran deeper...much, much deeper...and she wasn't about to examine it too closely. Not right now.

She smoothed her hands down her dress, making sure it was back in place and gave Dorothea an apologetic grimace. 'So sorry, Dorothea.'

'Don't you go apologising, that's the most exciting thing to happen on this island in for ever!'

Alaric snorted and Catherine's eyes shot to him—had he really just snorted? She laughed, the sound giddy and happy and so very easy. He looked young again, less tense, the brightness to his eyes, the colour in his cheeks...the warmth deep inside her spread, her feelings with it.

Feelings she really needed to get a handle on. But how could she when she was barely accustomed to feeling this way. Not even with Luke.

This was new. Intense. And for all she'd assumed it was the old merging with the new, she wasn't so sure. Something about Alaric now got to her, dug beneath her skin, had her losing her trusty control...

'Let me help you with that...' She hurried forward to aid Dorothea and quit the panicked direction of her thoughts.

Alaric filled her glass with the red wine he'd been enjoying on her arrival.

Catherine set the side dishes down as Dorothea lifted the main dish from the tray and rested it in the middle of the table, opening up the parchment paper and scrunching it around the dish. Steam rose up, filling the air with the most delicious scent, and Catherine hummed her approval, her eyes closing as she truly appreciated it.

When she opened them again, she caught Alaric watching her, his eyes soft, his expression unguarded, and she saw the same confusing fear that she was starting to feel deep inside. This connection between them had the power to break them if they let it…

She gave him a tentative smile and he followed her lead; the two of them stood there, smiling. An all-knowing Dorothea between them.

'I'll leave you both to enjoy your meal. There are more vegetables in the kitchen should you want any.'

'I think we'll be okay,' he murmured, his eyes not leaving Catherine's. 'You get yourself home.'

'I'll clean up after you finish, and then—'

'No, I'll take care of it…' He turned to Dorothea 'You take the leftover veg and kleftiko to enjoy with Andreas. Have an early night.'

'Well, you don't have to tell me twice!' She grinned as she nodded to them both. *'Kalispera.'*

'Kalispera—and take a bottle from the cellar with you too.'

'Oh, you really are spoiling us! Something tells me I have you to thank, Miss Wilde.' She gave Catherine a wink that had her blushing all over again.

'*Kalispera*, Dorothea.'

She watched the woman go, the air thickening the further away she walked and the closer they came to being alone again. She looked back at Alaric to find him watching her, the look in his eye making her stomach spin.

'What?'

'I'm just wrestling with reality.'

'Wrestling with reality?' She took up her wine glass and sampled it. Rich, dry and satisfying. Good choice. Though nothing beat the appeal of the man opposite her, looking at her in a way that made her pulse race. 'That sounds quite serious.'

'Oh, it is.'

'Tell me, which bit are you struggling with the most?'

'That you're really here, the great Kitty Wilde—'

'Don't call me that.' It blurted out of her, surprising herself as much as him, and she added softly, 'Please.'

'Okay. As I was saying, it's hard to believe that you're really here, and that we're really doing this.'

'Eating lamb kleftiko and drinking a very expensive—' she squinted at the bottle and smiled '—red Bordeaux?'

He laughed softly as he shook his head. 'Never mind the food and the drink. Do you have any idea how famous you are? How many men would do anything to be in my position?'

She shifted in her seat. 'Don't say that.'

'Why?'

'Because… Because you're not any man, and it makes me uncomfortable.'

'Uncomfortable to own your fame?'

'No. Not really. I just… I'm me when I'm with you. There's no pretence, no act, just me.'

He leaned forward on his elbows. 'Well, just you, how about we eat this and enjoy one another's company?'

She nodded, pleasure sweeping through her as she felt a common ground form for the first time since she'd arrived.

Food was finished. Dorothea's kleftiko was divine as always. His dinner companion…well, she was something else. Always had been, always would be.

And Alaric wasn't naïve. Out of practice, yes. But not naïve.

He knew where things were heading. He also knew it was a bad, bad idea.

He hadn't been with a woman in over three years. The idea of breaking that celibacy with Catherine was insane, foolish, asking for trouble. How could he ever hope to go back to his life as it was after she left?

And yet, every time she looked at him, as a man, a man she desired in spite of his scars, he lost sight of the bad and remembered the good. The connection they had when they were younger, the connection so ready to surface now.

'There's a little left, do you want it?'

He shook his head. 'You?'

She shook her head.

'Another drink?'

'What are you offering?'

'What do you fancy?'

With each question their smiles grew. 'I have champagne, dessert wine, ouzo, a raki?'

She pulled a face. 'Isn't that the drink that strips your liver?'

He laughed. 'I wasn't suggesting more than a shot.'

She grinned and his breath caught. She really was beautiful and not what he expected. Not that he'd known what to expect. Her mother, he supposed. A woman so focused on her career that everything else—*everyone* else—blurred into the background. But she wasn't any of that, despite what he'd told her. He knew she wasn't.

He also knew that her pushing him to discuss the past, to face it and change his outlook for the future, stemmed from a good place. She cared.

And he loved that she cared. He loved it too much. It's that which told him to keep his guard in place. The guard that was swiftly crumbling with the lateness of the hour and the growing sparkle in her eye.

'How about champagne?'

'Sounds perfect.'

He stood and started gathering up the plates.

She made to help and he took her hand, gave it a soft squeeze. 'I've got this. I don't want to risk you getting anything on that dress of yours.'

'What, this old thing?' She winked. 'Why don't you let me worry about that?'

He didn't even fight her on it, knowing full well that if she wanted to help she would, and the thought made him smile all the more.

They cleared the table and tidied the kitchen, making sure Dorothea didn't have much to do when she returned in the morning. It felt natural, *too* natural, to be doing such domesticated tasks beside her, but as they worked, she asked him about the origins of the house, and he stopped worrying about how it felt and concentrated on the details she wanted to know. The kind of farm it had once been, who had once lived here, how he'd discovered it…

But with every brush of her body against his, her perfume on the air, the sweet sound of her voice, it became harder and harder to resist pulling her to him.

'I take it you don't often clear up after dinner?'

He was reaching up into the cupboard for two champagne flutes when she asked, and he turned to look at her. 'Are you saying I don't look at home in my own kitchen?'

She pressed her lips together as her eyes danced. 'Something like that.'

'I'll have you know I do chip in on occasion,

but I don't like to tread on Dorothea's toes. That woman has a scowl that'll send a grown man running.'

Her eyes continued to dance. 'I can believe it, only…'

He folded his arms. 'Only?'

She nipped her bottom lip, a tea towel in hand as she dried off the casserole dish he had just washed, and the comforting sight coupled with the fire in his veins made his heart pulse.

'Domestic duties carried out by a man…' Her eyes trailed over him. Hunger. Desire. It was all there in the flush to her skin as she stopped drying the dish and took him in. 'A man as well built and rugged as you, I don't know whether to laugh at the strangeness of it or declare it the sexiest sight I've ever seen.'

He was upon her in two strides. 'Let me help you with that.'

He tugged the dish from her, the towel too, dumping them on the side with a clatter. 'That's not help—'

'I wasn't talking about the dish.' He wrapped an arm around her and bit back a groan as she came willingly, pressing her body up against his heightened state. 'I'm talking about the doubts you raise over my masculinity.'

Her lips parted with a soft 'Oh…' that he swallowed with his kiss. A deep, thorough, knee-buckling kiss that had him spinning her into the countertop as she clung to his shoulders, her nails biting through his shirt.

Her frustrated whimpers resonated off the stone walls, his desperate groans too. She curved her leg around him, urging him closer and closer still, but it wasn't enough. He needed more. He needed her all.

She tore her mouth away, her breath coming in pants, his shoulders heaving in tune.

'Is this what you do when a woman emasculates you?'

'If it's you, yes.'

She stared up at him, her cheeks flushed, her eyes hooded, and it was the sexiest sight *he* had ever seen.

'Alaric?'

'Yes?'

'Take me to bed.'

The blood rushed his ears, his core, his ability to breathe lost as she offered him everything he could want. Everything he'd always wanted. 'But—'

She pressed a finger to his lips. 'No buts... I'm not asking for more after tonight. I'm asking to satisfy this need between us before it gets out of our control.'

Out of our control...

He already feared they were long past that point but he couldn't stop it. Not now.

And he didn't want to.

CHAPTER EIGHT

CATHERINE FOLLOWED HIM down the stairs, scarce able to believe this was happening.

The small voice at the back of her mind persisted with its warning. Be careful. That the implications for him, for her, for their futures that were worlds apart, were huge and so she'd made it clear—she wasn't asking for more, this was about one night.

But to be his first…after three long years… it wasn't like he'd had anyone else come here…

Could it really be as simple as walking away after?

Her heart fluttered up into her throat, nerves getting the better of her, and as Alaric pushed open the bedroom door, she tugged him back to her. Kissed him until her head was dizzy with it and she could no longer think, she could no longer worry.

'I've forgotten the champagne,' he said against her lips. 'You get yourself comfy and I'll go.'

She shook her head, pulling him into the room with her, needing his thought-obliterating presence, his warmth, to keep out the warning, the reservation. 'No, I don't need champagne. I just need you.'

And she did need him, more than she'd ever

needed anyone, and it scared her as much as it reinforced her belief that this was meant to be.

'I like the way that sounds.' He lifted her up and she hooked her legs around his waist, their lips melding back together as though they'd never get enough. He backed her up against the bed, knelt on it as he lowered her down. 'Especially from you.'

And if he liked it, maybe he wouldn't object to her saying it more. Like every day for the rest of her stay and beyond. Could they continue this when her stay was over? Would it help him return to his family and the land of the living if she were to stay by his side for however long he needed? Could she do that? Would he want her to?

Her thoughts were as frenzied as the heat licking through her.

Stop thinking, she mentally berated herself, surrendering to his kiss, his touch, his body on hers. She kissed him harder, kissed him to mute her thoughts, kissed him to remind herself of what mattered right now…this.

He tore his mouth from hers, dragged kisses from her jaw to her ear and just beneath, where the sensitised pulse point made her whimper and writhe.

'This dress…it's killing me.' He caressed her through the fabric, his touch setting her skin alight. 'The way it looks against your skin, the way it feels…'

'It's a favourite.'

He murmured his agreement into the curve of her neck, his teeth nipping, his lips soft. He hooked his finger beneath one strap and teased it down.

'No bra too…'

Her insides quivered at the lustful heat in his voice, the thrill of what was to come.

'You really are killing me, Catherine.'

'If this is how dying feels—' she forked her fingers through his hair, watched him as he continued to unveil her '—I'd do it a thousand times over with you.'

It came out without thought, without reservation, and his eyes flicked to hers, passion blazing in their depths. She wondered if she'd said too much, overstepped an invisible line…panic pulsed through her, her fingers tightening in his hair.

'You and me both.' It was barely audible, a second's relief before the heat took over, warmth rushing through her core as he exposed one taut and needy peak to the cool air of the room.

She watched enraptured as he wet his bottom lip, the glimpse of tongue making her stomach clench, and he bowed his head, his breath sweeping over the sensitised nipple, his tongue following…

She gripped his shoulders, her nails clawing into his shirt as she arched into the caress, his name a moan on her lips. He cupped her breast, held her steady to his attention, his teeth grazing, his tongue flicking, his mouth sucking her in deep.

Pleasure surged fast and furious within her, her toes curling into the bed sheets as she grasped him like some form of anchor, fearing its intensity and revelling in it all the same. She pressed her head back into the pillow, clamped her eyes shut as she panted for air, cried out for more…

His hand fell to the tie at her waist, a bow the only thing holding her dress in place, and one sharp tug saw it undone.

'On second thoughts,' he murmured over her sensitised skin, 'this dress wouldn't be safe for the red carpet.'

'No?'

'No.' He rose up onto his knees, hemming her in with his thighs—it had never felt so good to be trapped. 'One wrong move and it's…'

He parted the fabric, uncovering her body to demonstrate his point, her small gold thong shimmering in the light as he hungrily took her all in.

'True.' Brazenly she lay there, goosebumps prickling over her skin, her nipples tightening further against the coolness of the room. 'But it does have its benefits for the after party…'

His eyes flashed to hers. 'This is the only after party I want to think about.'

She gave a soft laugh. 'Good. Now get back here.'

His grin was devilish as he dropped forward

and she pressed her palms into his chest, preventing him from getting any closer. 'Not so fast.'

She reached for the buttons of his shirt, undid one and felt the tension in his body swell exponentially, saw his jaw tighten, his mouth too. There was a sudden hesitancy in his gaze, a battle between desire and something else.

She wet her lips. 'What is it?'

'I'm not—it's not...' His head dropped forward and his eyes squeezed shut. 'It's not pretty, Catherine.'

'Pretty?' she teased softly, stroking her hand beneath his chin to bring his head back up. 'And you accused me of emasculating you?'

He opened his eyes and she smiled up into his gaze. 'I want you, Alaric.'

She saw his throat bob and his eyes shimmer.

'I want all of you...' Slowly she unbuttoned another, and another, all the while holding his eye. 'I want every scar that makes you who you are now... I want you.'

His breath shuddered out of him, his eyes blazing into hers as he kissed her deeply. 'You have me.'

Her heart pulsed, her fingers unsteady as she stroked the shirt from his shoulders, down his back, savouring the heat of his bare skin, the strength rippling beneath her touch. He rose up when she couldn't reach any further, tugging the rest of it away, and she couldn't breathe for the sight of him. He was everything. He *made* 'pretty' masculine. He was beautiful, sexy, magnificent, and *God*, how she wanted him.

He came back to her, his hands planting into the mattress either side of her, and she shook her head. 'Time to even out the power dynamic.'

He frowned and she shoved him, forcing him onto his back, and he laughed, the sound deep and husky and provoking the fire within.

'I should have known you'd want your way in the bedroom too.' He stroked at her bare thighs as she climbed over him, pulling her arms free of her dress and tossing it aside.

'Complaining?'

He stared up at her, his eyes so intense, so piercing. 'Not at all, princess.'

Princess. It didn't trigger a second's hesitation now. She loved that he had a name for her, loved that this was what he wanted too.

She lowered her hands to his bronzed chest, marvelling at the sheer strength beneath her touch, the trail of dark hair, the journey of scars that travelled down his side...

She leaned forward, her hair brushing against his skin. 'Do they hurt?'

His fingers flexed on her thighs. 'Not so much now, they're mostly numb.'

'Do you mind if I touch them?'

His throat bobbed, his laugh tight. 'You can do anything you like. I've told you I'm yours...'

For tonight, she silently reminded herself, pressing a light kiss to his cheek, tracing the silvery line. 'You're one hell of a specimen, Alaric, I'll give you that.'

Another tight laugh. 'I'm one scarred specimen.'

'So?' She met his gaze. 'They tell a story of your journey, your life…you shouldn't dismiss them, or hide them. Especially from me…'

She pressed a kiss to his collarbone, let her tongue caress the dip in this flesh—another scar, another piece of him. 'You are incredible.'

His nose flared with his breath, and his hands were so large as they lifted to hold her hips, but she wriggled free, dipping to take her desired tour of his body. She kissed every scar, caressed the silver lines with her tongue, her fingertips, showed him how beautiful he was, how strong, and sexy, and relished every groan he gave, every flex of his fingers, his body, as he succumbed to the pleasure she gave.

She reached the waistband to his trousers and rose, her fingers making light work of the button there, the zip too. She shimmied them away, his socks too, their shoes long gone in the journey from the kitchen to bedroom.

She stepped from the bed and his eyes followed her, her smile small. 'You lose yours and I'll lose mine.'

His eyes were dark, hungry, his smile carnal, and she didn't wait, she was too eager to please, too eager to watch his face change as she slid the flimsy fabric down her hips.

She straightened up and he shook his head. 'Catherine. You are…you really are going to be the death of me.'

'I hope not, because I really want this to last the whole night.'

His laugh was gruff.

'Never mind me.' She eyed his briefs. 'I'm waiting.'

He shucked them, the move so quick she squealed when he came at her, his hands on her waist as he pulled her back to the bed with him. He bowed his head to kiss her, her lashes fluttering closed as she wrapped her legs around his hips and positioned him just where she wanted him and froze.

'Protection!' She bit her lip hard, pushing back the thought that swiftly came next, the memory, the pain… 'Do you have any?'

He cursed and dragged in a breath. 'Not here.'

She sagged beneath him.

'But somewhere?' she said with hope.

He rolled onto his back, his palm pressing into his forehead. 'I'm such a fool. I have some but they pre-date my move here.'

She wrapped her leg around him, rested her head on his shoulder as her fingers trailed the curves and planes of his torso, her heart and breaths still racing with her need for him.

'Are you on the pill?'

'No. It doesn't agree with me.'

She moved against him, her disobedient body unwilling to stop, though her heart and head told her they must. 'Go and check them anyway. They might still be good.'

'Or we could just…satisfy ourselves in other ways…' He stroked his hand down her side, cupped her breast as his thumb rolled over her nipple, and she bit back a whimper.

'We could, only—' she kissed him, brushing the words against his lips '—I want to explore so many avenues with you that it would be nice not to worry about restrictions.'

He laughed as he pulled away and she watched him go, a smile playing about her lips, her heart light and free as she refused to let anything spoil this night—not the past, not the future, nothing.

Alaric opened the bathroom cabinet and took out the packet he knew he had. After all, he'd only relocated it very recently to make room for Catherine in the master suite. He hadn't expected to be getting it out again. In fact, he'd almost thrown them away, but the act had felt too final.

Too final? He wanted to laugh as he scanned the packet for a date, struggling to read as his hand shook with the realisation that they were really doing this…and then what?

How could they possibly return to how things were come morning?

Would she expect more? Would he?

Didn't this change everything?

It's one night of passion, came the voice of reason, no more, no less. The future didn't come into it.

But what of Fred? Did one night of bliss make him a traitor to his guilt?

Though surely he would suffer more for having known her, and let her go.

His gut rolled with the emptiness of it, his heart too quick to follow, and he pushed it all from his mind, projecting her instead—Catherine, in his bed, naked and waiting.

He closed the cabinet and caught his reflection in the mirror, the flush to his skin making his scars more garish. Was she crazy? How could she want this? Him?

The contrast between them couldn't be more profound and yet…she *did* want him.

He felt it in every caress of her fingers, her lips, saw it in her eyes and heard it in her voice as she'd made him feel worshipped…*him*.

And shouldn't he be the one doing the worshipping when he had her in his bed?

He strode back into the master bedroom to find her just as he left her. Naked, smiling, wanton.

'I was about to come and look for you.'

'Like that?'

She pushed herself up onto one elbow and gave a nod.

'Now I wish you had…'

He threw the packet down on the bedside table and joined her, his hand reaching out to cup her hip, to stroke at her skin that was so impossibly soft beneath his touch.

How long had it been since he'd touched a woman? His fingers trembled with the truth—too many years to count.

'Miss me that much?'

She leaned into him, her eyes worshipping him all over again. 'Too much.'

She hooked her leg over him, forcing him onto his back as she planted her palms into his chest and let her hair tickle at his skin.

'How long has it been for you?'

He frowned. Was she in his mind? 'A while.'

'Am I the first since you've lived here?'

He chuckled quietly. 'Do you see me hiding any other women here?'

Her eyes sparkled with his tease. 'You want to take it slow?'

He scoffed as he fought the urge to roll her back under him and demonstrate his answer. 'You know that conversation about emasculating me…'

Now she smiled. 'I don't want to be too much for you.'

'Right, that does it.' He rolled her under him,

relishing her squeal of delight as he covered her body with his. 'I'm taking the lead.'

He rolled his hips, her moan his reward. As was the surge of colour in her cheeks, her heavy-lidded gaze.

'I want you, Catherine. I don't need to go slow, I don't need your softness. I want this.'

'Then take me.'

He reached out for the packet and rose up, his eyes on hers as he sheathed himself and gritted his teeth against the rush within. Slowly he lowered himself over her, careful to keep his weight on his elbows as he kissed her, loving how she matched him move for move, her legs hooking around his hips, moving him against her.

'Are you sure, Catherine?' He had to ask. It would kill him to stop, but he would…

'I've never been more sure about anything. I want this. I want you, for however long I can have you.'

However long I can have you…

The words echoed through his mind as he took all that she was offering, all that made him feel so complete.

'Alaric!' She clung to his back, her eyes all vivid and blue.

'*You* are incredible.' He returned her compliment as he moved slowly, drawing out the sensation, controlling his need as he sought to build hers. 'You are beautiful… Caring… Kind.'

'Quit it, Alaric!' She clutched him tighter. 'You're filling my head with nonsense.'

'No.' He frowned, her reaction making him still. 'I'm filling it with the truth.'

She shook her head and squeezed her eyes shut.

'Look at me, Catherine.'

She refused and he stroked her hair back from her face.

'Look at me.' He cupped her face, held still until she opened her eyes, and when she did, he couldn't breathe. Her eyes were damp, wet with tears. His throat closed over, his voice hoarse as he assured her, 'You are all of those things and more, never believe otherwise.'

'More action, less words.' She tugged his mouth to hers, kissed him. 'I don't need the platitudes.'

'They're not—'

'Please, no more.'

What was this? His head told him to leave well alone, that whatever it was would only draw them closer together, but he couldn't. He wanted to understand. He *needed* to.

'Catherine, don't shut—'

She shoved him, forcing him onto his back as she tried to take control of the pace.

'Catherine?'

'Please, Alaric. I want this, I want you, no more, no less.'

'Talk to me.'

'No.' Her eyes pleaded with him. 'We're having sex. Fun. That doesn't need words.'

And yet she'd given him plenty. Made him feel desired, wanted, appreciated. Why wouldn't she let him do the same in return? Why did she look… *fearful*?

'What are you afraid of?'

It was his turn to ask the question.

'Nothing.' Though it caught in her throat and he held her hips steady, even as the demands of his body tried to override his heart and the need to hear the truth from her.

'Don't lie to me.'

'Please, Alaric, please.' She trembled in his hold. 'Let us have this.'

She fell forward, kissed him, her hands reaching for his and taking them above his head. He looked up into her eyes that were ablaze with so much and surrendered, giving himself over to her completely, letting her take her pleasure and deliver his own.

Tomorrow, they would walk away from this. They had to because the one thing he knew for sure—this couldn't happen again. He was drowning in her. Not steadily and slowly, not carefully or within his control, he was losing it.

He *was* lost. To her.

And that terrified him enough to keep his mouth shut and abide her demands, to let the thrill of what they were sharing in the now take over.

Because sex was finite.

It had an end.

And with it, this between them would cease to exist and life would be as it was. Safe. Steady. And wholly within his control.

No surprises. No fear. No guilt. No pain.

CHAPTER NINE

CATHERINE WOKE TO the smell of fresh coffee, the caress of the sea breeze across her naked skin and the sound of the waves rolling in the distance... bliss.

Her body ached in the most satisfying of ways and a smile was already on her lips as she untangled herself from the sheets and her lashes fluttered open. Sure enough, the glass door was ajar, a coffee pot was on the bedside table with two mugs, a jug of orange juice, glasses and glazed pastries. Oh, yum.

'Morning, sleepyhead.'

She rolled over to see Alaric stood at the foot of the bed, a towel slung around his hips, another hooked around his bare shoulders. His hair was damp, and his body still glistened from a very recent shower. If only she'd woken up a few minutes earlier, she thought, envying every small rivulet of water as it ran down his torso.

She took a second to catch her breath, another to try and moisten her very dry mouth. How could she want him so much already? They'd slept a few hours at most, the rest of the time they'd been hellbent on sating this never-ending hunger.

'I was beginning to think I'd have to rouse you.' He lifted the towel from around his neck to dry his hair, an innocent enough move, save for the fact that she was left watching his pecs and abs ripple, his arm muscles bulge… Definitely yum!

She swallowed, lifted her eyes to his that were so blue against his tan and the brightness of the room, and stretched out, aware of how naked she was. His eyes raked over her, projecting every salacious thought that mirrored her own.

He still wanted her.

But they were in unknown territory now…the morning after the most amazing night before.

Were they done? Or did the fact that she was still naked with his eyes feasting over her mean that they could pursue this a little longer because, seriously, if this was how good it felt the morning after, how good would it feel after a few days, a week, two…

She gave him a cat-like smile. 'And how, pray tell, were you hoping to do that?'

His eyes flashed, his lopsided grin hot. 'That would be telling.'

He rounded the bed to come up alongside her and stopped short, some unknown emotion flickering across his face as an invisible wall seemed to erect itself between them.

She opened her mouth to suggest her own possibilities fearing what was coming, but he got there first. 'We should talk.'

She felt her lips pout and she really wasn't the pouty kind. 'After coffee, yeah?' She pushed herself up to sitting. 'I'm no use to anyone without my morning hit.'

And she really wanted to live in the moment just a little longer…

He nodded, his smile small as he started to move away, and she reached out, hooked her fingers in the towel around his waist. 'I wasn't just referring to the caffeine hit…'

One sharp tug and he was on the bed with her, the towel in a heap on the floor, his naked body up against hers. And before she could declare herself triumphant, he was kissing her. She had known from the ease with which he'd landed beside her that he'd wanted it as much as her but to feel his mouth on hers sent her head spinning, her heart too.

'I knew I should have dressed before you woke up.' He brushed the words against her lips, his hands roaming over her as she raked her nails down his back.

'And spoil my fun?' She nipped his lip, playful punishment for the suggestion.

He hissed in a breath, taking up her hands, and threading his fingers through hers, he pinned them above her head. 'It's a good job I told Dorothea to take the day off, you're insatiable.'

'Funny, I was thinking the same about you.'

And then he was kissing her, so thoroughly that had there been any doubt remaining about what breakfast had entailed for him, it was obliterated now.

This was definitely her kind of wake-up call.

Almost an hour later, showered and dressed in a black bikini, she joined Alaric at the table outside her bedroom—or rather, *his* bedroom.

He'd made fresh coffee and whipped up some eggs, ham and slices of bread. The pastries had disappeared with their bedroom escapades and even the memory alone set off the heated flutters deep inside her.

'Wow, you really do know how to spoil a lady.'

He gave her the glimmer of a smile, his eyes not quite lifting to hers. 'If Dorothea found out I served just pastries for breakfast, she'd be beyond mad. Especially as she baked the bread fresh this morning and dropped it off on her way to the cove with Andreas.'

She smiled, her affection for the couple growing with each passing day. 'Sounds like they have the perfect day planned.'

She only wished theirs could be just as perfect.

Pulling out the chair across from him, she sat and took up her coffee, using its familiar aroma to try and soothe her churning stomach. The elephant in the room was about to make itself known and she really didn't want it to spoil the day. Not when it had been so very perfect from the off.

She planted her elbows on the table and hid behind her cup, sneaking a peek at him beneath her lashes as he squinted out over the pool to the sea beyond. She sensed that his furrowed brow wasn't entirely down to the brightness of the sun and she didn't want to prompt him into revealing his thoughts.

He flicked her a quick look, and another. She lowered her cup to the table and touched a hand to her damp hair, suddenly self-conscious in her un-made state. For the first time she could remember, she'd skipped her morning hair and make-up routine. Not only had she been too eager to be back with him, but he'd succeeded in making her feel comfortable, beautiful, desired just the way she was, and she hadn't felt the need for her protective shield…though now she was reconsidering it as he sent her another look, his eyes narrowing.

'What is it?'

'You're not wearing any make-up.'

A blush crept into her cheeks and she tried for a nonchalant shrug. 'I thought I'd go without. You know, for a change.'

His eyes trailed over her, their depths warming with his smile. 'You don't need it.'

She gave a flustered laugh, filled with a contradictory mix of both relief and anxiety. 'You had me worried for a second.'

She was still worried…

'I mean it, Catherine, you're beautiful without all that.'

Emotion clogged up her throat, his kind words

merging with those spoken during the night and making her wish this meant more, that it wasn't just a brief fling but a real, bona fide—

No, don't go there.

She picked up her fork. 'We should eat before these eggs go cold.'

'In this heat?' he murmured, knowing full well she was changing the subject.

'Humour me.'

He did but his eyes were still on her and she wet her lips, scooped up a healthy dollop of scrambled egg and popped it in her mouth. It was delicious—creamy and buttery, and *almost* the perfect distraction.

'This is tasty.' She covered her mouth as she complimented his culinary skills. Though to be fair she hadn't met a man yet who wasn't a pro when it came to scrambled, fried or omelette-style eggs. In nearly all pieces of romantic fiction, be it a book or a play or a movie, the man could always whip up a decent plate of eggs. The thought had a smile teasing at the corners of her mouth.

He eyed her suspiciously. 'What's so funny?'

'You don't want to know.'

Because she was pretty sure that if she told him what was really going through her mind, the unintended suggestion that they were living out their own romantic fairy tale right now, he'd baulk. Not that she wanted a relationship out of this. She *knew* she wouldn't get a relationship out of this.

So why couldn't she let them tackle the elephant and be done with it?

Maybe because you're lying to yourself...?

He took up his coffee, sipped at it, his eyes not once releasing her from their spell. 'Try me.'

She shook her head. 'Men and eggs. It's a bit of cliché.'

'I'm a cliché?'

'Not you, per se.' She laughed at his mock wounded expression. 'But you and the cooking up of eggs—yup!'

She was pleased to see the flicker of a smile even though she knew she was about to ruin it. She couldn't eat another bite without getting the impending conversation over.

'So… I've had my coffee, we've had our fun, let's talk.'

He struggled over the mouthful of food he had just taken, and she cursed her timing. Maybe he wasn't about to destroy everything after all. Maybe if she'd just kept her mouth shut, he wouldn't have raised it at all.

'Last night was…' He leaned back in his seat, his frown deepening as he held her gaze.

'Fun?' she suggested with an easy smile—she was supposed to be an actor after all.

'That.'

'But?'

He continued to watch her, his mouth lifting to one side and creasing at the scar tissue there. She had the overwhelming urge to ask if he'd applied sunscreen. Not that he'd appreciate the mollycoddling any more than she had when he'd asked her the same.

He swallowed and looked out to sea, his fingers raking through his hair that had dried wild thanks to the rough attention of her fingers not so long ago.

'You can just come out and say it, Alaric. It was a one night only deal, it was our moment to indulge, and now we're back to…what are we exactly?'

A silent pause and then he looked at her. 'Friends?'

Her mouth parted, her body fit to burst with the overwhelming rush of warmth—Friends.

After all he'd said they couldn't be again…

Now her smile was genuine, because for all she wanted more, more of him, more of this, just more, at least he wasn't rejecting her friendship any more.

And that had to be a good thing.

A very good thing.

'Friends?' Catherine's eyes shone back at him in the late-morning sun, her smile breathtaking. 'Now there's a turn up for the books.'

Her voice was a teasing murmur and he had the overwhelming urge to take her hand and drag her back to bed. He wanted her and would go on wanting her long after she left his island. He knew it, just as well as he knew this thirst would never be quenched.

Clenching his jaw, he looked back to the ocean. Barely a ripple broke the crystal blue surface and he tried to instil the same sense of calm within.

'Wouldn't you say?'

And of course she would press him on it. She was the most confident, most tempting woman he had ever known.

'Yes, Catherine. I know what I said the other day. But I'm hardly the sort of man to share the last twelve hours in bed with you and declare you no one to me.'

'Lucky me.'

He gave a soft scoff. 'I'm not sure lucky is the word I would use.'

'Well, lucky for you, I'm the one using it.'

And God he was smiling, a laugh brewing as he took in her bright smile, her eyes that he'd drowned in over and over during the night…this morning too.

He'd been a fool to cross that line with her and think he could come back from it unchanged. An absolute fool.

But given his time again, would he go back and do it differently?

Hell, no. Which likely made him an even bigger fool.

He started to dig into his food, a way to keep

his hands busy and her at a distance. Because he was just as hooked, just as in deep, even more so now he'd tasted her, felt that connection, felt how good they were together...how good it could be.

But they were friends, *just* friends, and he needed to get some distance between them again if he hoped to keep his heart safe and keep it that way.

CHAPTER TEN

As far as mornings-after went, Catherine deemed theirs as being rather pleasant overall. Civilised conversation, compliments exchanged, even some laughter along with an agreement that it had been fun but it wouldn't be repeated.

And the best bit—he'd declared them friends once more.

A bonus.

But five days later, she was forced to accept he'd only been saying what he thought she wanted to hear because Mr Elusive was back.

Each day he appeared less and less, in the gym, at the pool, for meals… He was ghosting her all over again and it was driving her to distraction. All the more so, because he'd *said* they were friends and she'd believed him.

She was annoyed but not so annoyed as to storm his study again. She didn't want to have to go to him. She shouldn't have to. And she refused to act needy for any man, particularly one that blew hot and cold and then ignored her so completely.

So she'd taken herself off to the trail for another run in the sun. Using the exertion and the oppressive heat to burn him out of her body and mind, not that it was working.

Thirty minutes in and she was *still* thinking about him.

Him and his smile. Him and his eyes. Him and his body and the amazing things he could do with it. More than that, she remembered the look on his face when he'd whispered all those sweet nothings to her and made love to her with— No, not made love...*had sex*.

Because making love...well, that was a different thing entirely, and she wasn't going there.

She swiped her sweat-banded wrist over her brow and turned the volume up on her earphones, using the music to drown out his voice and the images persisting in her head. She took in the beauty of her surroundings—the olive grove, the vibrant blue sea, the clear skies and the rocky path...

She was navigating a particularly uneven patch when the music cut out, replaced by her ring tone. She glanced at her watch. Kelsey. Her agent.

She slowed her pace and answered the call.

'Kelsey, what's up?'

'Are you...*exercising*? Please tell me you are, because with the way you're panting...'

She laughed and drew to a stop, hands on her hips as she sucked in a breath. 'I'm running and it's hot out here.'

'I make it four in the afternoon and you're running outdoors, in Greece, in the height of summer—are you crazy?!'

'A little.' She swiped her forehead once more,

squinted against the sun as she watched a distant yacht on the water. 'What is it?'

'I've sent you an email about your press appearances prior to the launch.'

She frowned. 'And you needed to ring me because…'

'Because I need to make sure you look at it.'

'I always keep on top of my email, you know that.'

'True, but…well…'

'Spit it out, Kelsey, it's not like you to beat around the bush.'

'It's Luke.'

'What about him?'

'Well, he'll obviously be there.'

'Ye-e-es,' she drawled, her frown deepening. 'He is my co-star, so I kind of know that already.'

'I know, but—well, I— I just wanted to make sure you're going to be okay.'

'Of course I'm going to be okay, when am I not?'

'It's just with all the press reports lately, what with your mother's opinion being splashed about, coupled with—'

'Wait, back up a step. What exactly has my mother been saying?'

'You haven't seen?'

'No.'

'But it's all over social media.'

'Charlie deals with all that. I've muted my notifications.' Charlie was her PA and a great one at that. She only bothered her when she felt it strictly necessary. And anything her mother was or wasn't doing was of no interest to her.

'Right, of course she does.'

'Do I really need to know?'

'It's just your mother being your mother. She loves the attention and siding with Luke over the suggested affair brings her a *lot* of attention.'

'She's done *what*?'

She could sense Kelsey's grimace at her outburst, but it stung. And she shouldn't be surprised, she shouldn't be hurt, but she was all that and more. Her own bleeding mother!

She took a stabilising breath and another.

'Kitty?' came her agent's soft prompt.

'Luke and I are fine, Kelsey.' She softened her voice. 'It doesn't matter what my mother has said, everyone knows we don't get along and anyone that matters will take her words with a pinch of salt.'

It was the truth. The entire world knew of her estranged relationship with her parents, her mother in particular, and no one knew of the baby she'd lost. No one save for Flo and Luke, and that was the only news she couldn't bear to be made public.

'Good. That's good. It will certainly make things run smoother in front of the camera if you're both on speaking terms still.'

'We're good. We're more than good.' Luke had been incredible, trying to reassure her, trying to help her, not once blaming her for the miscarriage...but she blamed herself enough for the two of them. 'Was there anything else?'

'The red carpet launch LA—who are you taking?'

She frowned again. 'I think the plan is for Luke and I to go together?'

'Really? You want to provoke *that* discussion when the focus of the press should be on the movie and not the status of your on-off relationship.'

She thought of what Alaric had said on the very same subject. 'Any press is good press, right?'

'And what if he wants to attend with someone else?'

'Then I'll go alone.' She was frustrated now, and she knew it was coming through in her voice, her elevated heart rate not helping matters. Thoughts of Alaric helping even less.

'Why don't I ask around, see who—'

'Good God, Kelsey, I don't need a date. I'm quite capable of standing there alone.'

'But so soon after—'

'Leave it, Kelsey. Please.'

'Very well.'

'Is that everything?'

'Yes—oh, no, wait! How is the script coming along? Do you think you'll be in a position for me to start pitching it soon?'

'Hopefully.' That was the one thing going to plan this holiday. Her frustration over Alaric had given her the impetus to lose herself in the pages and the characters she'd been burning to write about for years.

'Excellent. I'll let you get back to your run, then. Just be careful in that heat, yeah? We don't need you suffering heatstroke, or worse, coming back all lobster-like and peeling…there's only so much make-up can do.'

She rolled her eyes. Heaven forbid she did something that stupid for aesthetics' sake. Never mind the cancer risks…

She could just imagine how Alaric would react if he'd overheard Kelsey…if he even came close enough to overhear a conversation again. God, he was frustrating. Caring so much in one moment and pulling a disappearing act the next.

'See ya, Kels.'

'Bye, sweetie.'

She shoved her phone back into the side pocket of her running shorts and took off at speed now. Her frustration over Alaric mounting with frustration over Hollywood and its obsession with perfection, with appearances. She wanted to scream into the wind, keep going until all she could hear was the pounding of her heart in her ears, the music and—

The ground shifted beneath her, a rock coming loose as a jarring pain shot through her ankle. 'Argh!'

She flung her hands out to soften her fall, but she was already tumbling, stone and dirt breaking the skin as she left the path and sunk into the prickly dried-out undergrowth.

Her music went dead, the squawk of the birds she'd disturbed and the trill of the insects the only answer to her cry as she squeezed her eyes shut and hissed through the pain.

Great. Just great!

Alaric stared at the screens in his study but his ability to concentrate was waning.

Waning? Who was he trying to kid...? It had been virtually non-existent since Catherine's arrival. All the more absent since their one night together... The memory alone was enough to send his body into overdrive, the ache in his chest all the more pronounced.

The ache of *guilt* he assured himself because he knew it couldn't be anything else, he wouldn't allow it to be anything else. And he was being a jerk—*again*—so he deserved all the guilt he could throw at himself.

But then he'd tried to be normal, to be a friend. He'd tried to go about his daily routine with her in sight, but every glimpse and his pulse would leap, his body would warm, and he'd smile that ridiculous impulsive smile…and he'd known he was in trouble. So much trouble.

Because he wasn't pretending to be comfortable around her, he *was* comfortable. She made him feel accepted in his own skin, his new skin, and she slotted in here.

She fitted into his life in the most perfect of ways, and the desire to keep her, to want her to stay, was getting harder to resist. She made him forget his guilt, she made him forget everything but the way she made him feel, and he knew that was wrong, so very wrong.

And so he'd avoided temptation altogether. In all likelihood she would detest him by the time this trip was over and then—

'Kyrios de Vere!' The door to his study burst open and a flushed Dorothea appeared, her hands gesturing frantically. 'Come quick.'

He frowned, launching himself out of his seat and striding towards her. 'What is it?'

'It's Miss Wilde. She's had a fall, a nasty one.'

He cursed under his breath, his pulse spiking as he followed her out. 'Where is she?'

'Andreas is helping her back. He phoned ahead asking me to get you.'

'*Back?* Where's she been?'

'Running.'

He cursed again, felt the heat of the late-afternoon sun beat down on him as they emerged from the house and took a right, to the start of the trail, and… His chest contracted. There she was, hobbling, her arm hooked around Andreas' shoulders for support, her entire body covered in dirt, her running bra and shorts offering no protection at all. She was cut, grazed, her face, her knee, her ankle…

Another stifled curse and he was racing forward, the emotions he'd been working so hard to suppress rising with such force they were choking up his chest.

'What am I going to do with you?' He loomed over her and she glared at him, at least that's what he thought it was meant to be, but the small cut to her lip made it more of a pout and the hiss she gave told him the effort had cost her.

'I'm fine, thanks for asking.' She stared straight ahead. 'You can go back to your work.'

Andreas gave him a look and he stepped in. 'I'll take her.'

'You. Will. *Not.*' She hobbled back, her eyes glistening as she spoke, her rejection cutting deep, but he had to help her. He *had* to.

Closing the distance she'd created, he swept her up in his arms.

'Alaric!' She shoved against him. 'Put me down this second!'

'Quit it, princess.'

It was hurting her to speak. It was hurting him to see her in pain. Why did he feel like even this fall was his fault?

She harrumphed, folding her arms, her body tense in his hold, but at least she wasn't pushing him away now. He snuck a peek. She looked mutinous. Her eyes shooting darts in the direction of an innocent Dorothea as she hurried towards them.

'She's sprained her ankle, I think,' Andreas said to Dorothea. 'She'll need to get it raised and get some ice on it too.'

She nodded as she fell into step beside them, tutting away. 'I knew all this running out here was a bad thing.'

You and me both.

He gritted his teeth, his jaw pulsing with the effort not to say it as Andreas ran ahead to hold open the front door. He strode on in and headed for the stairs.

'I'll take her down to the bedroom. She'll need cleaning up. Can you bring the first aid kit, Dorothea? The ice pack and a glass of water too.' He looked down at her sweat- and dirt-stained face, feeling her pain like a crushing force within. 'Did you not even take a drink with you?'

She flicked him a look that quite accurately depicted the middle finger gesture and he bit back a relieved laugh. Feisty as ever.

'You can hate me all you like, but I'm not leaving you until I know you're okay.'

She mumbled something incoherent under her breath, but before he could ask, she started to tremble in his hold—shock. He held her tighter, wishing he could do more.

'Bring me a whisky too, Andreas.'

The man's brows hit the ceiling.

'It's not for me,' he explained, though he had a feeling he'd be wanting one too, very soon.

Andreas nodded and raced ahead as Dorothea branched off to the kitchen.

'This really isn't necessary,' Catherine grumbled through her teeth that were now chattering incessantly.

'I'll be the judge of that.'

'Dorothea and Andreas are more than capable of taking care of me.'

'You're my guest, you've got hurt on my watch. I'll be the one taking care of you.'

'So now I'm your guest.' She shook her head, grunted. 'You're the most confusing, contradictory man I've ever met!'

'And you're the most frustrating and stubborn woman, so I reckon we're even.'

She glared up at him. 'If you weren't carrying me down concrete steps right now, I'd… I'd…'

'What? Slap me?' He gave her an amused look that only riled her further. 'It's a good job I'm carrying you, then.'

Another emphatic harrumph and then she rested her head against his shoulder, and he forgot the reason she was in his arms, he forgot the reason he'd been hiding out, he forgot everything but the feel of her. The sense that she felt so right there, curled up against him, his arms around her, protecting her...

'I have it all,' Dorothea called down the stairs, her footsteps quick to follow as she hurried after them.

'And I have the whisky, two glasses too, just in case,' Andreas said, joining them.

'Thank you.' Alaric strode into the bedroom, making for the bed.

'You can't put me on there like this.' She started to wriggle against him. 'I'll ruin the sheets.'

He ignored her, placing her down as gently as he could. 'Dorothea, fetch a bowl with fresh water and ice please.'

'Of course.' She placed the items she'd brought down on the side table and left to get the rest.

'Do you want me to pour?' Andreas held up the whisky and glasses.

'No, it's fine. I can take it from here.'

He placed them on the side table. 'Is there anything else I can get?'

'Not right now. I'll call if we need anything.'

He nodded and looked back at Catherine, his face creased up with concern. 'You're in good hands, Miss Wilde.'

She gripped her arms around her middle and gave him a watery smile. 'Thank you, Andreas. For everything.'

Dorothea came bustling in with a bowl, cloths

and a towel, placing them down on the foot of the bed. 'Right, let's get you cleaned up.'

Alaric touched a hand to hers. 'It's okay, I've got this.'

'Well, I'm not sure if...' She looked at Catherine and back at him, her hesitation obvious, and he gave her a smile.

'I'm quite capable, I promise.'

'Well, okay, if Miss Wilde is happy.'

Catherine didn't look happy, folded up like she was, knees bent, her head dropped forward, but as she looked up at Dorothea, she gave her a nod and managed another smile.

'Very well, call if you need anything else.'

'We will.' He watched her leave with Andreas, waiting for the door to close before looking back to Catherine and then the whisky. He uncorked the bottle and poured a small measure in both. 'Here, take a sip—it'll help with the shock.'

'I'm not—'

He stared her refusal down, shoving the drink into her hand and grasping her other to place both around the glass. 'You are. You're shaking.'

Dubiously, she eyed both him and the drink but took a disgruntled sip, wincing as the alcohol caught the cut in her lip.

'Is this you making up for the fact you've barely been near me since the other night?'

He reached over her and took up the spare pillows, careful not to knock her as he did so and planting them midway down the bed.

He took the glass from her hands. 'Lay back.'

She didn't move, just looked at him expectant. Waiting for the answer he wasn't going to give.

'Come on, Catherine, you need to get that ankle elevated and iced… Unless you want to find yourself immobile for even longer.'

Her lashes fluttered, the internal debate clear in her glistening blues but eventually, she lay back and gingerly lifted her leg into his awaiting hands. He looked at her ankle, the swelling already apparent near the bone, and fought to keep his expression blank.

'I'm just going to take your trainers off. Let me know if I hurt you.'

She scoffed and he flicked her a quick look. She wasn't scoffing about the potential pain from the sprain, she was scoffing about the pain he'd already inflicted.

'I'm sorry I've not—' carefully he unthreaded the lace on her trainer, loosening off the straps '—been around much.'

'Avoiding me, more like.'

He lifted the heel of her trainer, his other hand holding her calf steady and taking the weight. 'I guess.'

'You avoiding me warrants an *"I guess,"* not a denial, an extra apology.' She cursed.

He knew she was lashing out and why. She had

good reason. He was the one in the wrong and she deserved an answer, an explanation. 'If I said I needed some distance between us, would it make you feel any better?'

She frowned. At least she'd stopped shivering but the way she was looking at him now was worse. Like she could see him for what he was—a fool, a man who knew she was too good for him, would always be too good for him, and yet cared for her anyway.

He focused on her foot instead, slowly easing the trainer away and lowering her leg to the pillows. He checked to make sure her ankle was higher than her heart and then removed her other trainer and sock. All the while he could feel her watching him, her curiosity mounting.

'You know, it's just a sprain. I can take it from here.'

'Not until I have you cleaned up. Your cuts need tending to.'

He took up the ice pack Dorothea had brought and curved it around her injury, trying not to wince when she did but feeling it all the same.

'Sorry,' he murmured when she gave a sharp gasp.

'*That's* not your fault.'

No, she was right there too.

'You can go now, Alaric, please.' Her eyes glistened with fresh tears—tears he knew she was refusing to let fall. 'I'm not some child who needs looking after. I can clean myself up.'

He wasn't leaving. If he had his way, free of the accident, free of the guilt, he'd never leave her. Ignoring her protests, he wrung the cloth in the bowl of clean water and brought it to the knee closest to him.

She hissed, her eyes watering all the more, her glare evident behind the tears. 'Please, Alaric, you're going to ruin the bedding too.'

'Do you think I care a damn about the bedding, Catherine?!' He shot her a fierce stare, knowing his inner torment was written in his face, in the thickness to his voice. 'Just lie still.'

He turned and picked up the whisky. 'Here, have some more. It'll help.'

She didn't move, her eyes mistrustful and tearing him apart.

'Please, Catherine, let me take care of you.'

She took a shaky breath, her lashes lowering as she reached out for the glass.

'Thank you.'

It came out so quiet and the tension between his shoulder blades eased. The relief in his heart so very evident.

He rinsed the cloth as she took a sip and gave another wince.

She touched a finger to the cut and cringed. 'I must look a sight.'

He looked at her, really looked, and he couldn't

say what he truly thought. That even with a fat lip on the rise, bloody and wounded, she still looked beautiful. Beautiful and vulnerable, and it was a lethal mix to his defences.

He took her hand from her face, touched the cloth to her lip and tried to ignore the way it made him feel, the way she watched him beneath lashes that clung together with her tears and tried to understand him.

'It's a clean cut at least...' His voice was thick, raw, as raw as his heart felt. 'But I think you'll have a lump there for a few days.'

He reached for an ice cube from the tray Dorothea had brought and wrapped it in a small cloth. 'Here, hold this over it.'

She didn't baulk, just placed her glass down and lay back into the pillows, her eyes to the ceiling as she held the wrapped ice to her lip, her other hand resting on her bare torso. Carefully, he tended to every cut, every graze, the tension in her entire body giving away her continued pain and discomfort.

By the time he'd finished, she looked ready to sleep, and as he brushed her hair back from her eyes, he gave her a small smile.

'I'll send for Dorothea and she can help you change. You look like you could do with some sleep.'

Her brows drew together, her blue eyes swirling with so many questions, so much emotion, he could feel her reaching inside him, silencing his voice, immobilising his body...

And then she blinked and looked away. 'Thank you for taking care of me.'

It was a whisper, so sad and defeated, and he wanted to reach for her, to say anything, do anything, to make it all better. But where did he even begin?

The problems were his, not hers.

'Just go, Alaric. Please.'

Fresh tears welled in the corners of her eyes and he fought the urge to wipe them away. He wanted to climb on the bed, pull her to him, whisper all the sweet nothings raging in his head, his heart, and hold her safe.

And it was that deep-rooted need that had him clearing up the debris and striding for the door. 'Call if you need anything. Dorothea will be straight down.'

'Not you. Got it.'

He could just make out the words said under her breath and forced himself to keep moving and not look back because he knew if he did he would cave. And he'd only end up confusing their relationship more, hurting her even more in the process.

And above all, he wanted to protect her, even if that meant protecting her from his messed-up self.

CHAPTER ELEVEN

CATHERINE LIFTED HER gaze from her laptop to see Dorothea crossing the poolside, straight for her. *Uh-oh, here we go.*

She lifted the brim of her straw hat and lowered the lid of her laptop to smile at the woman in the hope of softening whatever admonishment was coming and wondered what it was this time. She wasn't putting weight on her three-day-old injury and she was lathered in sunblock. She was being a good patient and she was getting some actual writing done. All was good with the world... well, almost.

'Your shoulder, Miss Wilde, it is in the sun!'

She looked to the left, to the right. Sure enough the sun had moved just enough to expose the tip of her shoulder, but she'd been so engrossed in her script she hadn't noticed.

'Oops, I'll just...' She shifted the laptop, made to rise, and Dorothea practically squeaked.

'You stay right there!'

The woman was already at her side, tilting the parasol to cover all of her once more.

'Maybe it is time you came inside?'

'I like it out here—the view is inspiring and it helps me to focus.' She'd been out there most of the day, the pool taunting her just a bit as she craved a decent swim, but three days into her injury, it was still too tender.

'Is there anything I can get for you?'

She gave Dorothea a smile. 'A new ankle?'

'Aah.' Dorothea's eyes softened, her smile full of sympathy. 'It'll be as good as new before you know it…so long as you continue to rest it properly.' The last she added in that matronly manner of hers and Catherine could feel her cheeks blaze.

Guilty as charged…

She'd been caught at least a dozen times already, trying to go about her day as normal, and each time she'd earned herself a stern ticking off from Dorothea or Andreas, even the distant glare from Alaric the one time he'd caught her trying some very early morning yoga. Very early because she'd hoped to avoid being caught. Yoga because there was nothing much else she could put her body through, and she was an exercise addict. She had to be. Her metabolism alone didn't keep her this trim.

'I'm trying, I just hate being so idle.'

'Me too, so I understand, but still, rest—*nai*?'

'*Nai.*'

'Now, lunch—what can I get you?'

'I'm fine. I'm still full from breakfast.'

She eyed her sceptically. 'Fruit and yogurt is not enough for the whole day.'

'I'll get something later if I'm hungry.'

'You said the same yesterday.'

'I wasn't hungry.'

'And the day before.'

She frowned up at her. 'I wasn't then either.'

Dorothea tutted under her breath. 'You'll waste away.'

Hardly. Though she kept the thought to herself. No exercise meant no calorie burn, which in turn meant weight gain. She'd already gained enough during her time on the island thanks to Dorothea's fabulous cooking and she couldn't risk any more. She had a red carpet movie premiere just around the corner and a dress that was made to fit like a glove. She absolutely could *not* put more weight on.

'I'm fine, honestly.'

Dorothea nodded but the severity in her expression didn't lift. 'You call if you need something bringing out. You're not to climb those stairs, understood?'

Her heart warmed in her chest as she stared up at the woman who treated her more like a caring mother than her own ever had and a genuine smile touched her lips, along with the surprising prick of tears.

Perhaps the emotional turmoil of the past year was catching up with her—*and perhaps you're more hurt by Alaric's avoidance of you than you care to admit?*

'Understood, Miss Wilde?'

She swallowed, refocusing on Dorothea. 'Perfectly… Thank you.'

'You're welcome.'

She watched her go, her mind awash with all that had happened since her arrival. She could see why Alaric chose to stay here. He wasn't as alone as she'd first feared, as alone as his sister and family believed him to be. Dorothea, Andreas, even Marsel, were more like family than staff. Aside from their respectful forms of address, they cared for him and vice versa.

They cared for her too. It was obvious in their warm brown eyes that lit up with their laughter, softened with their compassion and narrowed when they were cross with her for pushing her body too far too quickly. Yes, even when they were giving her a ticking off, she knew it came from a good place.

She shook her head and opened her laptop fully again, ready to get stuck into the adventures of her heroine, Maisy, once more. At least the script was going well. Having bed rest forced upon her meant there wasn't much else she could do to fill her time. And now she had a thorny plot issue to fix. How to get Maisy from the—

'Catherine! What the hell is wrong with you?'

Her eyes snapped up, the man striding towards her immediately dominating her vision and setting her pulse racing. Did he *have* to be so goddamn sexy *all* the time?

'Good afternoon to you too, Alaric.'

He shook his head, pausing at the foot of her sunbed, his hands fisted on his hips, his white tee straining across his chest…did he own T-shirts in any other colour because she'd yet to see him in one. Black would look good, maybe a soft grey…

'I'm kind of busy working so if you have something to say, just come out and say it and then we can both go back to our jobs.' She smiled sweetly. He was, after all, the one who was always too busy to spend any real time with her. The least she could do was return the favour.

'Dorothea says you're not eating properly.'

'Dorothea is worrying unnecessarily.'

He crossed his arms. 'So, you haven't been skipping lunch and surviving on fruit and yogurt all day.'

'No, I've eaten dinner too.'

'According to Dorothea you're only eating a fraction of what she serves up.'

Heat started to unfurl deep within her gut, and it wasn't the good kind. 'Alaric, you're not my moth—' She stalled. Her mother wouldn't care, her mother would be pleased that she was starving herself because she couldn't exercise it off. 'You're not the boss of me, you don't get to come out here and give me a ticking off.'

'I'm not giving you a ticking off.'

Her brows nudged the rim of her straw hat.

'Okay, I am. I'm just… I'm concerned, Catherine.'

'Well, don't be. Now if you don't mind…' Pointedly, she went back to her screen, though tuning him out was nowhere near as easy. Even his cologne reached her now, its rich woody scent teasing at the fire inside that was supposed to be all anger. Only it wasn't. And hell, that served to frustrate her more.

'Where would you like me to put it?'

Dorothea? She peered around him to see the woman returning with a tray of…

'Alaric!' She glared up at him. 'I said I was fine.'

'Tough, we're having a late lunch together.'

'We are not.'

'We *are*—' He broke off, looked away as he raked his fingers through his hair and took a breath before coming back to her, the effort to compose himself obvious. 'Sorry. Please, will you come and have some food with me?'

'Why?'

'Because I'd like to spend time with you.'

She laughed, the sound practically delirious. Did he really think she would cave that easily? That she would believe him even?

'Please, Catherine. I've been an arse, but I'm worried about you. I'm not going to force you to eat if you don't want to, but I would like to spend a little time together.'

'You would?' It sounded as dubious as she felt.

'Yes.'

'So, it's not because you want to make sure I eat something.'

'Can't it be both?'

She studied him intently, feeling her heart flutter in her chest as she saw how much he cared and remembered that he didn't, because he couldn't get away from her fast enough most days.

'I've missed your company.'

It was a raw confession, honest even to her dubious ears, and it cost him to admit it, but it cost her heart more. 'Okay.'

The beginnings of a smile flickered around his mouth, the sexy fullness to that lower lip, the dip in the middle of the top...if she closed her eyes, she'd remember how it felt to kiss them too. She'd also remember how he'd looked at her, with passion and something so much deeper blazing in those blue eyes, something that they hinted at right now.

'Thank you.' His smile widened and he turned to Dorothea. 'The table outside the bedroom is perfect. It's in the shade.'

She closed her laptop and set it down, swinging her legs over the edge of the bed. She shouldn't have agreed, she should have made him suffer like she had, but having him concerned for her made her feel...it made her feel too much.

She pushed herself up and limped forward.

'Oh, no, you don't.' He was by her side in an instant.

'I can walk! Granted, it's awkward but I can manage.'

'What's the point when I'm here to carry you?'

'Whoa, whoa, whoa…' She shook her head, waved him down. 'Help is one thing. Carrying me is—'

Too late, she was already up against his chest and it shouldn't feel good. It really, really shouldn't. But there was something about his strength surrounding her, the warmth of his body against hers…she gave an involuntary little shiver as she revelled in it.

'Are you—*cold*?' He eyed her incredulously.

'Don't be ridiculous.'

Her cheeks flamed and she pinned her hat in place as she hid behind its brim, her inability to act around him making them burn ever deeper. She was Kitty Wilde, an award-winning performer, but with Alaric she was Catherine. There was no facade, no act, just her…exposed, raw and utterly susceptible to him.

Maybe that was the problem.

She was herself…she couldn't hide.

No matter how much he pushed her away.

Alaric only had himself to blame. He was the one that had insisted on picking Catherine up, holding her to him, feeling the connection between them pulse and grow.

He'd been the one determined to step in as

one look at Dorothea's face when she'd returned from the poolside to report the exact same news— Catherine isn't eating properly—had urged him to his feet, ready to do battle. Ready to throttle her mother too, but that was an age-old anger, an age-old fight he'd never been able to have outright.

But this, he could.

He glanced down to see her still tucked behind the brim of her straw hat and his frown deepened. Already she'd lost weight, and that wasn't healthy. You didn't lose weight that quickly unless you were sick or on some unsustainable diet. And it was most definitely the latter.

He lowered her onto a seat at the table. 'Are you comfortable? Do you want me to get another chair to raise your ankle?'

She shook her head without looking up. 'No, I'll be fine. It's been elevated plenty this morning.'

'When did you last ice it?'

'About an hour ago.'

'Would you like me to get—'

'Enough, Alaric!' Her eyes shot to his. 'Please sit down and stop fussing.'

He did as she bade, his frown unmoving though.

'So, this is what it takes to get some attention from you? A fall and a busted ankle?'

He set a plate before her and started dishing up the Greek salad Dorothea had prepared and gave her a smile full of forced tease. 'A bit extreme, wouldn't you say?'

'Don't flatter yourself. I certainly didn't do this on purpose.'

'No? I'm not so sure.' He continued with the teasing, desperate to lighten the mood and not get caught up in the look in her eye, the proximity of her bikini-clad body, the kimono she favoured doing nothing to conceal every inch of her appealing body.

'Funny, Alaric, very funny.'

He started slicing off a piece of fresh baked bread.

'No bread for me,' she rushed out.

'But it's still warm from the oven, you'll love it.'

'I'll love it too much, that's the problem.'

He shook his head at her. 'That makes no sense.'

He cut it anyway and placed it on a plate beside her salad. 'In case you change your mind.'

He served himself too, discreetly watching as she took a bite of salad and chewed it over, her eyes on the ocean. How did he broach it with her? It wasn't healthy not to eat, but at the same time, who was he to judge her, to criticise. She was right to say it wasn't his place and yet…

'Stop it.' Her eyes were still on the view.

'Stop what?'

'Stop looking at me like that.'

'I'm not looking at you like anything.'

'Right?' Now she turned to him, her brows drawn together. 'So, you're not judging me, then?'

'If you think I'm judging you, then it suggests you believe I have cause to.'

She shook her head, her lips twitching as she forked up more salad.

'I get that it's hard for you right now,' he tried softly, 'not being able to stick to your workout regime and—'

'What would you know of it?'

'I know you spend almost as many hours keeping active in some way as you do not.'

'And how would you know that when I hardly see you around?'

'I know, Catherine.'

'What?' Her laugh was harsh. 'Do you have cameras dotted about, keeping an eye on me? Is this actually a heavily guarded fortress and you use those computer screens of yours to watch the island's movements?'

'Stop trying to deflect.'

'I'm not.' She dropped her fork. 'Okay, I am. But I don't want to talk about my exercise and eating habits. What I want to talk about is you. I want to talk about Flo and the fact you're going to be an uncle. I want to talk about you coming back to the UK for a visit.'

His blood ran cold, her quick-fire change in focus making his stomach roll. 'We agreed not to talk about it.'

'We agreed not to talk about a lot of things, and I consider my diet very much out of bounds.'

'Your *diet* isn't sensible.'

Her cheeks flared, her lack of make-up making every flush far more evident, every expression far more pure and real, reaching under his skin, right to the very heart of him. He fisted his hand on the table, urging it all away.

'My *diet* is logical. If I'm not exercising, I'm cutting the calories I take in.'

'There's cutting what you consume and then there's not eating. You're inching towards the latter.'

'I'm eating now.'

'Only because I made you.'

'You *encouraged* me. You can't make me do anything I wouldn't do of my own accord.'

His chest eased a little. 'Good…but you can't deny that you love Dorothea's bread, and one slice isn't going to hurt you.'

'A moment on the lips, a lifetime on the hips,' she sing-songed.

'And now you sound like your mother.'

She paled in an instant.

'Hey.' He frowned. 'I was joking.'

'No, you weren't.'

'Well, can you blame me?' There was no use denying it—he'd been joking to an extent but what he'd said was true. 'She used to say it to you all the time. Family barbecues, weddings, birthday parties… If she even caught you looking at dessert, out it came.'

'Yeah, well, she was right to an extent.'

'Why was she right? Why do you have to worry about it so much?'

'Are you really asking me that when you know what I do for a living?'

'And what about body positivity? I thought that was all the rage now.'

'It's Hollywood, Alaric, it'll never change.'

'It will if the people within it change.'

She stared at him for a long moment and he started to think he was getting through to her, making a difference. 'Be that as it may, I still have to get into my designer dress for a movie premiere in a month's time. If I put on even the slightest bit of weight it won't fit.'

'So, get a new dress, you can afford it.'

'It's not that simple,' she choked out with a laugh. 'Do you know how in demand fashion designers are? We're booked in months in advance for the perfect outfit. It doesn't get thrown on last minute.'

He shrugged. 'Your fans, the press, they want to see you, the person in the dress. What does it matter what designer you're wearing, other than the fact you're putting money in their pockets by promoting their wares? Now there's an idea—you could go to an unknown for an outfit, elevate them to your level, rather than throwing money into the same few pockets.'

She tilted her head to the side. 'That's an idea I

actually like, but still…even an unknown doesn't pull something off last minute.'

'Then you wear something off the hanger.'

Another choked laugh. 'Absolutely not.'

'Why?'

'Because it's not the done thing.'

'So what?'

'You really don't get it, do you?'

'Oh, I get it. But what it tells me is that all that talk about you not seeing me for this—' he ran the back of his fingers down his scarred cheek '—but who I am inside is bull.'

She frowned at him, her head shaking, her hand reaching out. 'That's totally different and you know it.'

'Do I, Catherine? Because if I listen to you right now, if I look at your actions over the last few days, the eating like a bird, testing your foot long before it's healed, your desperation to keep up appearances, it all becomes a lie. Ultimately, *you* care. Ultimately, it's all about how one looks.'

'In Hollywood, yes. But it's not me.'

'Right, Hollywood.' His laugh was harsh. 'And you and Hollywood are two separate entities.'

'Yes.' She shook her head. 'No. You're twisting my words.'

'You're beautiful, Catherine.'

'See!' She thrust a hand at him. 'Now you're just proving my point!'

'No, I'm not.'

'You are! Telling me I'm beautiful. It doesn't come easy. I work hard to keep myself looking like this. I deprive myself of the foods I like, I work out, I… I…'

She stopped as he shook his head. 'You're beautiful on the inside, Catherine.'

Her laugh was more a scoff. 'That old cliché.'

'Cliché?' He frowned at her, knowing full well he had her. 'But isn't that what you were trying to tell me the other day? That you, my family, they don't see me for my scars, they see who I am underneath?'

Her lips parted but no words emerged.

'Or did I misunderstand?'

'Of course you didn't,' she said softly, folding her hands in her lap. 'I meant everything I said.'

'Just like I meant everything I said in bed the other night, when I told you what I thought of you.'

She opened her mouth, closed it again, pursed it off to the side as she looked to the ocean once more, but he could sense the cogs were turning, that she was processing all he had said. That he had effectively used her own words against her. And it was risky to bring that night up again, the connection they'd shared coming to the surface, but this was more important than the protective wall around his heart.

'Okay. Okay. You win. I get what you're saying.

My problem is that Hollywood is my home, not literally but in terms of my career it is.'

'And look what it did to your mother?'

She flicked him a look and he was surprised to see the hint of tears welling, her mother evoking such a deep reaction once more.

'You know how hard I've tried not to become her? That every day it's there as a mantra and still…' She shook her head. 'She creeps in, you know. But I wanted to be an actor. I wanted… I thought I could do it and avoid her mistakes…'

'You were always one for the stage. I don't think you would have been happy doing anything else.'

'Maybe.'

She looked so lost in her own world that he started to regret even pushing her as far as he had, but he wanted her to see it, needed her to see it. 'Honestly, Catherine. So what if you gain a few pounds? So what if you wear a dress off the hanger, or something from an unknown? You're still you. You're still the person who brings characters to life on the big screen, brings joy to people's lives—tears, sadness, happiness.'

The flicker of a smile crossed her lips. 'I'd like to be seen as more than that though, more than beauty over brains. I want to be the creator behind the scenes, I want to write the words that inspire such passion, I want to do more.'

He smiled in the face of her strength, her dream.

'And you will. I meant it when I said you put your mind to something, it happens.'

'I wish I could bottle you.'

He chuckled, feeling the tension in the air lift. 'I'm not sure I'd like that.'

'I would, then I could uncork you every time I doubted myself.'

She smiled at him, and for a second, time stood still, the world fell away. If only things were different, if only the accident hadn't happened, if only their worlds were compatible…

And then she lowered her gaze to the plate with the slither of bread he had cut and took it up. 'It does look lovely.'

'You don't have to eat it,' he assured her. 'I just didn't want you to deprive yourself because you think it will in some way go against you.'

She laughed softly. 'It is just a piece of bread after all.'

'Hey, not just any bread. Dorothea will be down here with the rolling pin if she hears you say that.'

He offered her the small bowl of olive oil and balsamic vinegar to dip it in and watched as she scooped it to her mouth, her hum of appreciation making him want to groan too.

She chewed it over, catching a little drop from her chin with her finger and licking it clean. 'You know what this means though?'

He was so caught in the movement of her finger, her lips, it took a second for him to register what she had said.

'What's that?'

'You owe me a talk about home.'

Silently, he cursed. He'd walked straight into it, but...

'Lucky we have plenty of days left for that.'

'Is this you saying you're done hiding away?'

He gave her a tight smile. 'I don't really have a choice if I'm to make sure you rest that ankle properly and eat sensibly.'

'Ah...' She tore a piece of bread off and popped it into her mouth, her twinkling blues giving the impression of a gleeful child. 'So true.'

Tiny flutters erupted deep within his gut. 'I'm beginning to think you really did do this on purpose.'

'You'll never know, Alaric... I am an exceptional actor after all.'

He almost glanced at her ankle to double-check it was most definitely bruised and stopped himself. It was enough to still see the cut healing on her bottom lip...another part of her anatomy he really shouldn't look at but for a very different reason.

'Very funny, princess.'

CHAPTER TWELVE

CATHERINE SQUINTED OVER at Alaric sitting at the table outside her room, a book in hand, while she lounged under the parasol with her laptop. As promised, he'd spent nearly every waking hour within viewing distance, rarely getting close enough to provoke the persistent chemistry between them, but close enough to keep his eye on her.

And her, him.

She loved watching him unawares, free to look her fill without him knowing, free to take in the unguarded expression on his face. Over the past few days, she'd found herself doing it more and more, as though she was trying to imprint the memory in her brain so that when she left this place, she'd remember this moment and all the others.

And she hadn't given up hope yet of coaxing him off the island. Flo had messaged that morning to ask how it was going and she'd given her an honest answer—things were improving.

Because they were.

She hadn't told her that the reason was down to an injury she'd sustained, and it had forced him out of hiding. Flo didn't need to know that. And with her friend's pregnancy hormones she'd only go into over-protective mode and hop on a plane herself, a luxury she could readily afford, especially as she'd taken early maternity leave due to the concerns over her blood pressure. And she didn't want to be aggravating that either. So no, she told her everything was in hand and that she was slowly working her magic.

Magic which she really needed to be getting on with. She caught her lower lip in her teeth as she pondered her opening line…she didn't want to spoil the common ground they had found. A way to co-exist without him fleeing.

But she had less than a fortnight to change his mind.

'Out with it.'

She jumped at his low command, issued into the pages of his book.

'Beg your pardon.'

She felt her cheeks flush as he lifted his head, her breath catching as his piercing blue eyes met with hers, heating her from across the distance. 'I reckon you've been watching me for at least a chapter.'

'I have n—' His brows nudged up, a small smile playing about his lips, and she quit her denial, closing her laptop with aplomb. 'I fancy a swim.'

'You sure that's wise?'

'I won't know until I try.' She swung her feet to the ground and sat up. 'Could you help me to the pool, please?'

He watched her slip the kimono from her shoulders and she made sure to draw out the move as she spied the pulse working in his jaw. No, they definitely hadn't lost the spark. If anything, it had intensified with each passing day as they remained in one another's company and tried to fight it, to deny it.

'Of course.'

Closing the book, a thriller judging by the cover, he got to his feet and averted his gaze as he approached. She wondered if his heart was now racing in tune with hers, anticipation of their closing proximity making it hard to think straight.

She stood before he reached her, testing her weight on her ankle and finding it wasn't so painful if she was careful.

'It's not too— *oh*!' He'd wrapped an arm around her bare waist, taking her weight and making her insides thrum in one.

'You were saying?'

She wet her lips and looked up at him. If she was honest, she wasn't quite sure any more. His touch had done its usual task of clearing her head of all thought. And she should be used to it with him helping her everywhere and no longer avoiding her. But there was no getting used to the force of their attraction, or the way his eyes seemed to penetrate her very soul when he looked at her like he was now.

'I was saying...' She looked down and eased

her foot forward, using him for support as they made their way to the pool edge. 'It's not too bad today.'

'Good.'

A breeze caught the brim of her hat, blowing it free, and her hand shot up, but he beat her to it, grabbing it and bringing his body around, his front facing hers as he caught both her and her hat and...*oh, my*.

She was pressed right up against his chest, his hand clutching the hat to her back, his other arm locked around her waist.

'Perhaps it's best we leave the hat here.' His voice was thick, low, and he made no attempt to move, no attempt to ease the closeness, to lift the moment.

She nodded, not wanting to risk anything else. Was he going to kiss her? He *looked* like he was going to kiss her...especially as his gaze fell to her mouth, the blue of his eyes drowned out by the lascivious dark and sending an excited jolt straight through her core. 'How's your lip?'

'It's—it's feeling much better,' she breathed, her tongue sweeping briefly across the said body part, easing its sudden dryness while teasing him too.

'Good...' It vibrated through him, his arms flexing around her.

'Alaric?'

He shook his head. 'Don't.'

A frown touched her brow. 'You don't know what I was going to say.'

'I can see it in your face.'

'And I can see it in yours.'

He shook his head. 'You're impossible.'

She gave the smallest of laughs, making her body vibrate against his. '*I'm* the impossible one.'

She could tell he was fighting a grin, could tell he was fighting the pull between them too, but he twisted to toss her hat onto the bed and tugged her towel over it to stop it blowing away. 'Come on, you said you wanted a dip.'

She wanted so many things in that moment and a dip definitely wasn't one of them.

It didn't matter if it was wise, or sensible, she wanted him. And the more time they spent together, the more the connection between them swelled and the more she felt his barriers fall.

She let him lower her to the edge of the pool and she did the rest, enjoying the cool water on her flushed skin as she looked up at him. 'You going to join me?'

'Are you going to behave?'

'Hardly.'

And then he laughed, the sound so glorious, so easy, so different to how he'd been when she'd first arrived, and hope bloomed warm inside her chest. Hope that she could convince him there was more to life than just his island, that he did deserve to live, really live…

She watched as he stripped his T-shirt and tossed it aside, dropping into the water beside her, his eyes finding hers both wary and warm. She reached for his hand and pulled him towards her, saying nothing as she closed the distance between them.

If she didn't try, she wouldn't get...

His eyes fell to her mouth and she did the same, her intent clear, hope soaring as he didn't pull away, hope soaring even more as she reached up, a hand sliding into his hair, her mouth sweeping against his...

'Catherine, this isn't a good idea.'

'It feels like a very good idea.' She dragged the words against his lips, felt his breath shudder through him, heard the groan deep within his chest, and then he was lifting her against him. Hard muscle against pliant flesh. He forked his hand through her hair, tugging her head back to deepen the kiss, his tongue delving and tangling with hers. It was explosive. Like a switch had gone off inside him, inside her...

The water sloshed around them as he backed her up to the wall of the pool, her legs wrapped around his hips, the heat within enough to contend with the sun blazing down.

He tore his mouth away, sucked in a breath as he pressed his forehead to hers, his hands deep within her hair. 'I've wanted to do that for days.'

'You *should* have done.'

He shook his head, his eyes searing hers. 'This can only get messy, Catherine. I don't want to hurt you. I don't.'

'Who's getting hurt? Not me? I'm not asking for a future. I'm not asking for more than my stay here. And I'd much rather spend it like this than constantly fighting it.'

She kissed him to add to her point, kissed him deeper to convince him, kissed him until he was kissing her back harder and more fiercely than she...then she tore her mouth away. 'Now tell me you want to fight this.'

'Hell, no, we're going to bed.'

What is the definition of insanity?

His mind pushed the question as they lay on the bed, naked. A white sheet drawn to the waist, his arm wrapped around her as she lay her head on his shoulder, her leg entwined with his.

The perfect moment.

Aside from the uneven beat to his heart as he considered the answer, knowing full well he was the very epitome of it.

Doing the same thing over and over again and expecting a different result...

In his case, succumbing to the chemistry between them again and not expecting the mark she left on him to grow.

Though maybe it wasn't insanity at all, maybe it was stupidity, because he knew where this would lead. He knew he was falling in deeper and deeper with her. He knew he'd have to fight harder to fend off the belief that this was possible, real, a relationship with a future.

'What are you thinking about?' She snuggled in closer, her head tilting up as her eyes searched out his.

He met her gaze with a smile that not even his worries could quash. 'I'm wondering how soon we can go again.'

'Liar.' She nudged him softly with her hip. 'Though I do approve of your answer.'

He chuckled, his fingers caressing her side as he looked back to the ceiling. He could quite happily lie there for the rest of the day, the week even—work, food, be damned.

'Can I ask you something?'

The loaded question pulled his body taut…so much for being content. 'Of course.'

'Why don't you paint any more?'

She shifted her head to eye the brightly co-loured canvas above the bed. 'You're so talented.'

'Was. I *was* talented.'

She frowned at him. 'And you can't paint now?'

'I can't paint, I can't draw, I can't sketch.' He flexed his fingers on her hip, felt the constant tightness there. 'Not like I used to.'

She lowered her gaze to his hand, turned it over. Her fingers delicate as she traced the scar there. 'Have you tried recently?'

'No.' It came out gruff, partly with the pain she'd stirred up, and partly with the shiver her caress triggered.

'From where I'm lying, they still feel pretty talented to me.' She lifted his hand to her lips, kissed his palm softly. 'You should try again.'

He was about to refuse when she looked up at him. 'What does it matter if the work you produce has changed, it doesn't make it any less. You enjoyed it because it felt good for you to create, you enjoyed that time with just you and your canvas. The number of times I would visit when we were kids and you would be in a flurry of creativity, with that wild look in your eye. Almost like a mad professor.'

'A mad what?' He was laughing but this was news to him.

'You know, the nutty professor look—crazy hair, even crazier eyes?'

'Oh, cheers. Very attractive.'

She gave a dainty shrug, her smile small. 'I quite liked the look on you.'

He shook his head, pulled her in closer.

'You shouldn't stop creating just because your work is different now.'

'You'll have a hard time convincing the artist in me of that.'

'But it was therapy for you, creating back then. It would serve the same purpose now....and so what if it's different. Doesn't it make it special in its own way?'

He gave a soft scoff. 'To be reminded that I can no longer do something as well as I used to.'

She lowered her gaze to where her fingers played with the hairs on his chest. 'It's all subjective. There's no such thing as a perfect piece of art, just as there's no perfect book or movie or performance. Who cares if it's not as good in your eyes, if you come to get the same enjoyment out of creating it?'

He stared down at her, heard her words so perfect, so right. No perfect performance…he'd take his hat off to her now, throw her roses on the stage, because what she'd said made *perfect* sense. Sense he hadn't seen before. And he couldn't speak, only hold her closer as the emotion inside swelled.

Fear of not being good enough had stopped him from creating. Fear of the man he was now had stopped him leaving the island. Fear of being resented by his late friend's wife had stopped him from talking to her and dealing with his guilt… but now, with Catherine wrapped up in his arms, he didn't feel afraid any more, he felt capable of anything.

Ready to take out his sketchpad, ready to return home, ready to speak to Cherie…

Through her wholehearted acceptance of him, she'd crept beneath his barriers. Teaching him to embrace the man he was now, not fear it, or loathe it.

'Is this what you had in mind when you agreed to come here, to my island?'

'What?' She pushed up on his chest. 'Seducing you?'

'Luring me into your bed to fill my head with possibility.'

She laughed softly. 'The truth?'

He nodded, loving how her eyes sparkled down at him.

'I wanted to see you. Absolutely, I did. It's been so long...' Her lashes lowered, a second's avoidance as she seemed to withdraw into herself and then she looked at him again. 'I wanted to see how you were for myself and, of course, I wanted to convince you to come home once in a while. I also needed to escape my life...' She closed her eyes, her body trembling against him and exposing that pain again. Pain that revolved around Luke and it was like a knife twisting deep inside him.

'As for getting you into bed *per se*—' her eyes opened, locked with his, and her sudden smile almost had him forgetting the hurt that preceded it '— the second I saw you again I will admit to wanting all of the above.'

'You're totally serious, aren't you.' It was a statement, not a question. He was long past doubting her attraction.

'Err, yeah! All those feelings I had for you when

we were kids, teens, imagine that and then being confronted by you now…your bad-boy vibe has a whole lot going for it.'

'My bad-boy vibe?' He choked on a laugh, grabbing her hand to press it to his scarred cheek and hold it there. '*This* gives me a bad-boy vibe?'

Her eyes shimmered into his. 'Hell, yeah.'

She eased her hand from beneath his, to trail it along the scar, her eyes alive with the heated direction of her thoughts, and he flipped her under him, so fast she cried out.

He started to roll back. 'Your ankle! I'm s—'

She cut him off with a kiss. 'My ankle is fine!'

And just like that he was perfecting insanity again.

CHAPTER THIRTEEN

A KNOCK AT the door woke Catherine in an instant and she shot upright, the bed sheet clutched to her chest, eyes wide.

"Alaric!' she whisper-shouted. 'Alaric!'

She shoved him and he grunted, wrapping his arms around her waist. 'What's the emergency?'

'There's someone at the door.'

He squinted up at her, raising his hand to ward off the light from the bedside lamp as she thrust it on. 'What time is it?'

'I've no idea. Late.' Very late, judging by the pitch-black outdoors and the very vocal sounds of the nightlife coming through the small gap they'd left in the sliding door.

The knock came again, followed by Dorothea's voice. 'Miss Wilde… Kyrios de Vere?'

She swallowed. Okay, so that cat was out of the bag…not that it had ever really been in considering her and Alaric had been inseparable for the past week, working together, eating together, sleeping together…ever since their silent understanding to enjoy this time while they could. Not that much sleeping had gone on which explained why they'd fallen asleep in the afternoon and the day had disappeared on them.

'I've brought food,' Dorothea called through the door. 'I thought you may be hungry?'

Alaric chuckled into her hip and she shoved him again.

'Well, she's not wrong.'

'It's not funny.'

'It is a little funny. And she's right, we could do with some food.'

She started to move off the bed—

'You can come in, Dorothea.'

And flung herself back, the sheets clutched to her chest again, as she threw him a mutinous glare.

He chuckled all the more, pushing himself up to sitting and settling back against the headboard, pulling her in closer as the door opened. A blushing Dorothea strode in, eyes averted, her tray out in front of her and loaded with a variety of food.

'I brought a selection as I wasn't sure what you would prefer.' She slid the tray onto the bedside table. 'Now what can I get you to drink?'

'Water would be lovely,' Catherine replied, surprised her voice sounded far more composed than she felt.

'And some…champagne?' Alaric looked at her for approval and she felt her cheeks burn further, her 'yes' more of a squeak as she thanked Dorothea.

'You're most welcome.' Off she went, happy to be on another errand, happier still to see them in bed together, Catherine was sure.

'I can't believe you did that.' She gave him another playful shove and he pulled her back against him, his grin heart-melting, his eyes alive with mischief, and then he kissed her. A long, deep kiss that had her limbs softening, a fresh wave of heat consuming her as her head emptied out.

'She knew anyway,' he murmured against her lips.

'So? We could have at least put some clothes on.'

'Are you kidding? That's not going to bother her. She's just happy to see me acting like a normal, healthy man again.'

'You mean *virile*?' she teased, the sexual undercurrent building with ease.

He laughed. 'That too.'

She shook her head, her smile uncontainable. It was so easy to lose herself in him, in these days where the outside world couldn't intervene and everything felt so…perfect.

He leaned away to reach for a plate. 'You'll love these.'

She took in the neat pile of glistening vine-covered rolls he offered out to her. 'Ah, dolmades.'

His eyes widened in surprise.

'Hey, I am well-travelled, you know!'

'Clearly.'

She leaned forward, took one up and cupped her hand beneath as she bit into it and licked her lips to scoop up the remnants.

'Nice?'

She chewed it over, the taste explosion divine. Rice, dill, lemon, mint—yum!

She swallowed it down with a nod and a hum.

'Tell me how you're not the size of a house when you eat like this every day,' she teased, offering him a bite.

He laughed before taking it from her fingers with his mouth, chewing it over as his eyes danced. 'Like you, I train hard to balance it out.'

'That makes me feel better. It would suck if you were this trim and got to eat all you wanted without having to put in any effort.'

'Would it now?'

'Yup. Take it from a woman who knows the pain of exercise.'

He smiled at her. 'Ready for another?'

She nodded and he picked one up, pulling it away from her lips at the last second.

'But don't expect me to let you hop on the treadmill tomorrow—that ankle still has to heal.'

'Duh.' She stared into his eyes as she quickly pinched a bite. 'I'm not that stupid.'

His brows nudged upwards.

'I'm not!' She devoured the rest of it before adding, 'Or at least I was, but not now—not any more.'

'Because?'

'Because I'm beautiful on the inside.' She rolled her eyes and gave a laugh, but it caught in her throat. His eyes were on fire, stubborn, insistent, as he forced her to be serious.

'I mean it, Catherine.'

'I know you mean it.' She reassured him softly and he took up her hand, kissed it as his eyes lifted to hers.

'Just remember it...'

He held her eye as he pressed another kiss to her hand and she mentally added for him, *When we're no longer together*.

'Remember it?' he urged, the unsaid words hanging in the air between them, and she nodded.

'You know...' she whispered, her voice trapped in her chest as her heart beat wild with her feelings for him, feelings that were way out of her control, regardless of the untold pact that this would be over when she left. 'You could come visit and remind me as often as you liked...'

'Is this you trying to convince me to leave my island again?'

'Maybe...is it working?'

He shook his head but there was a smile in his eyes. 'You have shown me there's more to life than hiding out here, I'll concede that.'

She leaned back, surprise making her drop the sheet that was covering her modesty, and as his eyes dipped, their naughty gleam threatened to distract her.

'Behave!' She palmed his chest. 'Are you serious?'

He tugged his eyes from her nakedness, and it wasn't salacious heat burning into her now, it was his sincerity. 'Yes, you've shown me to accept the man I am now, to live and laugh again. You've given me hope that I can go home to my family, that I can contact Cherie and try to put it behind me, to move on in some way.'

'You don't deserve the guilt, Alaric.' Her voice was soft but no less vehement. 'You've suffered enough.'

'Perhaps.'

'Are you serious, or are you just humouring me?'

His smile lifted to one side. 'No, I'm not just humouring you. And yes, I'm serious. I'm not looking forward to it. I'm apprehensive about how Cherie will be, I'm apprehensive about how my family will receive me, hell, I'm apprehensive about being out in public at all, but...'

'Those you don't know don't matter, and those that do will love you all the more for coming back to them.'

His eyes softened, his smile too.

'And you're going to be an uncle, Alaric, that's exciting, special. Flo's been going out of her mind worrying about you.'

'I know.'

'But do you know her blood pressure is already through the roof, that she's been forced to take early maternity leave?'

He frowned. 'No. She never said…she…' He looked away, raked his hand through his hair with a curse. 'Why didn't she say anything?'

'I don't know. I guess because you've had so much going on it didn't seem fair. Or maybe she thought you'd see it as her way of guilt-tripping you into coming home again and didn't think that fair either.'

'I knew she'd been out of the office more, I just hadn't… I didn't…' He leaned forward, his knees coming up to rest his arms on them, his head hanging forward. He cursed again. 'I've been so wrapped up in my own world… How could I have been so selfish?'

'You weren't selfish.'

'No?' He rolled his head to look at her.

'No.' She placed a gentle hand on his back. 'You were suffering. And they understand why you left, granted they don't understand why you've stayed away, but when you explain, they'll get it. They'll just be happy to see you again.'

'I see my father regularly.'

'On a screen, Alaric, that's hardly seeing him. And even then, it's all business, isn't it?'

'What more would we talk about?'

She gave a soft scoff. 'Feelings! We all have them unless you're a robot and I *know* you're not. You care, you just like to pretend you don't.'

He said nothing and she stroked his back that was so tense beneath her touch. 'It's not too late, you know. The most important thing is that you're going to go back. They love you and they'll be ready to welcome you home, when you're ready to go there.'

She snuggled into him, forgetting all about the food as she lost herself in their conversation and the milestone they'd hit. 'It'll all work out, I just know it.'

He turned, pressed his lips to her hair. 'I like your optimism.'

'And I like you.'

It came out easily. Honest. And it hit home once more, just how much she liked him and just how much this had to be temporary because for all she denied being like her mother, her actions over the years had told a different story…her actions had told her just how selfish and messed up she was, and she would never expose Alaric to that side of her.

Never.

But what if she could do better? What if she could learn from the past and pave the way to a better future? One that allowed her to love, to be loved, to have it all?

But Alaric didn't know what she had done.

Alaric didn't know what had truly gone down with Luke.

Alaric didn't know just what a screw-up she was deep down and the idea of telling him, of cracking herself open and confessing…

And didn't that make her a nasty piece of work, when he was opening himself up to her, his insecurities, his worries, and still she hadn't told him the truth.

It crushed her inside, crushed her all the more as she accepted that she didn't just like him, she loved him. That she was *in* love with him, and she had to tell him the whole ugly truth. She owed him that at the very least.

She straightened up, drawing her knees to her chest, the sheet too. 'There's something I need to tell you, something that very few people know.'

His head snapped up. 'Are you okay?'

She couldn't answer.

'Are you sick?'

She shook her head. 'No. Not in the way you're thinking.'

He leaned forward, seeking to hold her eye, but she couldn't look at him. 'Flo knows and Luke… I haven't told anyone else.'

He reached out for her, but she leaned away. 'No. Just let me… I need to get this off my chest, and if you hug me, I'll lose the ability to speak…' Her throat was already clamping closed, the well of emotion rising so sharply she couldn't draw a full breath.

He sat back against the headboard and she didn't need to look to know how wary his gaze had become. 'You know you can tell me anything, Catherine.'

She nodded. She did. But first, she needed to get it straight in her head. And she needed Dorothea to come and go again so that she could be sure there would be no interruptions because, once she started, it would all come spilling out, and then, who knew where they would be…

She was quiet for so long that he wondered if she would say anything at all and then Dorothea returned with the drinks and he realised she'd been waiting for them to be alone. Properly alone.

He poured a drink, one of each, and offered her them both.

She took the water while he favoured the champagne. Not that he felt ready to celebrate anything, it was more to ease his nerves that were fraught with whatever was coming.

'You understand my relationship with my mother better than most. My relationship with my father too. What there is of it.'

'Back then, yes. Not so much now.'

She nodded but said nothing more and he pressed, 'Do you see them much?'

'No. Not particularly. Mum never got over me hitting A-list status. Once she realised my growing fame didn't help her with the roles she was being offered, things turned nasty pretty quickly, and to be honest, I think she'd had enough of playing at family. They divorced soon after and Mum left to be with her latest toy boy and Dad…well, he fell into his own pit of despair and no matter what I did, what I said, he just…'

She gave the smallest of shrugs and his heart ached for her. There he was avoiding his own family who'd always been there for him, when she couldn't even hold the attention of hers.

'He just didn't care. Worse still, I look like her, so seeing me is just a constant reminder of his loss.'

A fire burned in Alaric's gut, his hands fisting as his dislike for the man took hold. He was her father, for Christ's sake, and instead of focusing on what he did have—the love of his daughter— he was so wrapped up in the callous wife he'd lost.

'Anyway, when Luke and I got together it was a whirlwind. It happens like that on set, you know. You're so wrapped up in the characters you're playing that the boundaries blur and before you know it, you're an item. And it's easier that way, dating on set. It's virtually impossible to find time to date outside of it, and we were happy, in our own way…'

She gave him a sad smile and looked away, her eyes lost to the outside world, her sadness, her pain, and his heart caught in his chest.

'I never wanted to become my mother, Alaric, I didn't. And so I found it easier not to get caught up in relationships in the first place, not to feel the pressure of dividing my attention between my work and my loved ones. I figured it would all come later, right? That I'd get to a point in my career where I was content and ready to settle down.'

'But then you met Luke?'

She gave a small nod.

'What happened?' he asked even though the question had goosebumps prickling over his skin. He didn't think he could bear it if she confessed her love for another man, her heartache even…

'I got pregnant.'

The blood drained from his face, shock assaulting him like a punch to the gut. 'You were…' He cleared his throat, tried again. 'You were *pregnant*?'

She shuddered as she took a breath, her eyes flitting to him so very briefly, but he couldn't miss the torment, the sadness, the pain.

'Yes. It wasn't planned. It was the last thing I expected—we expected.' Her voice cracked with emotion, her arms wrapped tight around her legs, the knuckles of the hand closest to him glowing white as she gripped her elbow. 'We were always careful, always used protection, but…but it failed.'

She started to rock, and he didn't dare move, not until he felt she was done.

'I took the morning-after pill—we had no choice. But it—it didn't work. A few weeks later I knew I had to take a test. I didn't feel any different, but I was late. Luke was beside himself, excited with it. He was talking of a future, full on, like it was all a done deal, and I…'

She cleared her throat, her voice so quiet when she spoke again. 'I was terrified. I wasn't ready. It wasn't the right time. I cared for Luke, I did, but a baby…' She shook her head, her body rocking all the more, and he could see the tears building, sense the effort it was taking for her to hold them back.

'What did you do?'

'Nothing. I did nothing.'

She turned to him now, her lower lip trembling, the tears in her eyes overflowing as they ran down her cheeks. 'I lost it. I didn't want it, and then it was gone, like it had never been.'

'Oh, Catherine…' He reached for her and she leaned away.

'Don't. I don't deserve sympathy. Don't you see, I was as bad as my mother in the end. I had a life growing inside me, I was a mother and I—I wished it away.'

'There's lots of reasons to lose a baby, but it never comes down to someone wishing it away, Catherine. You know that.'

She shook her head, stared at him. 'Do I?'

'Of course you do.'

'Luke said the same. He was so good to me, so sweet, but I didn't deserve his kindness… I didn't.'

'Of course you did, you were hurting and—'

'But he knew I wasn't ready. He knew I didn't want… I didn't want…' She couldn't finish and he couldn't stop himself reaching for her. He pulled her to him and this time she came, curling up against him as he rocked her, soothing every sob that wracked her body.

'It wasn't your fault.' He kissed her hair. 'It wasn't.'

'I couldn't marry him. I said yes because of the baby, because I thought it was the right thing to do. And when I lost the baby, I just… I couldn't go through with it."

'I'm sure Luke would have understood, Catherine. He would have been hurting, just as you are now.'

She sniffed, swiped her palm across her cheeks as she leant back to look up at him. 'I wasn't ready.'

He cupped her jaw, his thumb sweeping over her damp cheek. 'I know, princess.'

'But I—when I lost it, I broke down. I would have given anything to have that time again, to have nurtured it, treasured it. I wanted to be a mother. I wanted to wish away my career and have my baby back.'

Have her baby back *and* Luke? Was this more than just agony over a miscarriage? Was it agony over the only real relationship she'd ever had?

'I'm sure if you went to Luke and spoke to him, he would understand…' He forced himself to say, 'You could still have a future together?'

She frowned through the tears, her head shaking. 'I don't want Luke, I never *loved* Luke.'

His heart pulsed in his chest as her eyes widened into his, so much on show if he was willing to see it. 'What I felt for him is a fraction of what I feel for you, what I've always felt for you, Alaric.'

He clutched her tighter, pulled her up to his chest and sucked in a breath. 'You've got me, right now, you've got me.'

She shuddered against him. 'But don't you see, I'm just as bad as my mother.'

His laugh was tight, incredulous. 'I don't know how you can think that.'

'I wished away my own child.'

'You were blindsided by a pregnancy, that's very different to abandoning your own flesh and blood, Catherine.'

He continued to rock her, stroke her hair, kiss her head, wishing life could be different, that they could somehow merge the two worlds in which they lived to make them compatible.

'I'm ready now, Alaric. It's the reason this script is so important. It's not just about proving I'm more than just Kitty Wilde, the actor. I want my life back. I don't want to be a prisoner to twenty-four-seven filming schedules, PR appearances, interviews... I love film, I always want to be in film, but on my own terms and on the other side of the lens.'

'It sounds like you have it all planned out.'

He could feel the resolve building within her, the strength seeping into her limbs as she pushed up off his chest. 'I'm thirty now, it's time I took control of my life and made room for the people that I love.'

'Flo will certainly be happy to see more of you.'

'And you?' Excitement thrived behind the tears still glistening in her vivid blues. 'Could we see each other more?'

His chest contracted, his body icing over with the impossibility of it. 'I'm not… I know I've said I'll visit home, that I'll speak to Cherie too, but you…me and you—' he couldn't look at her as he finished '—we just don't work outside of this island.'

'You don't know that.' She reached out to touch her palm to his cheek, urging him back to her. 'I've never met anyone that makes me feel the way that you do, Alaric. It's always been there between us, but these past few weeks…it's changed everything. And I know you feel it too.' She lowered her hand to his heart. 'I *know* you do.'

'It doesn't matter what I feel, Catherine.'

He clutched her fingers, his intention to remove her touch, but he couldn't drag them away. He was lost in her gaze swimming with such passion, such confusion, and the contact, no matter what had driven him to stop it, felt unbreakable.

'Why?'

'You and I can't have a relationship.'

'And I repeat…' She sniffed, using the back of her free hand to swipe away more tears as she raised her chin to him. 'Why?'

He couldn't respond. His head was a mess of words, of sentences that didn't make sense, feelings that he couldn't identify, string together, make coherent.

'This feels different to me, this feels special,' she pressed. 'I haven't felt this way about anyone, and… I don't want to make another mistake. I don't want to be my mother. And you tell me that I'm not, so let me prove it, with you.'

'I'm not the man to prove it with, can't you see that? I don't belong in your world.'

'What world?'

'Show business. Hollywood. Being in the public eye. I can't do it, Catherine. Look at me. Can you imagine the tabloids, the cover stories that would appear?'

'Yes…' It came out as a whisper. 'And I wish I could protect you from it. I wish I could say it won't happen, but you and I both know it will. It doesn't mean we have to live in fear of it, that we should give them the power to keep us apart. I don't care what they say, I only—'

'You *should* care.'

'My mother would care, Alaric, and that's not me…or is this *you* proving you don't mean what you say?'

'Don't question my honesty, Catherine. I have never lied to you, and I have let you in. But I can't give you what you deserve.'

'And what is it you think I deserve?'

'The dreams you speak of…the award winning actor-cum-screenwriter. It doesn't matter that you'll be on the other side of the screen. If you go after your dream, you will still be on the red carpet, you will still be in the public eye, you will still be famous. As you deserve. But not with a broken man by your side.'

'You're not broken, Alaric.'

'I'm damaged goods to them.'

She might not find him so horrific, his family might not either. As the queen of appearances, she'd convinced him that he could return to his family and be seen once more, for who he was beyond the scars. And yes, he had the strength, the confidence, to accept who he was now.

But to stand alongside her in the very public eye, the difference so very marked. It would be the subject of every tabloid, the cover story of every gossip rag, the very epitome of Beauty and the Beast, and the press would go wild for it.

It didn't matter that she didn't see him like that, they would.

And to have his happiness splashed across the tabloids, rubbed in the face of Fred's family, Cherie, their child… It was one thing to return, but that…

'So, this really is it?' she said quietly. 'We have this time now and then it's over.'

'It's what has to happen.'

'Not if we don't want it to, not if you feel the same way I do.'

'How can I possibly know how you—'

'I *love* you, Alaric.'

His heart squeezed tight in his chest, warmth exploding out and dousing just as quick.

'I loved you in my teens, I love you all the more now. I know I'm not the best judge of it, not after how my parents were or how they treated me, but I know I don't want this to end, that I want to keep you as part of my life. I want to share the highs and the lows and be there by your side. And I have *never* felt like that about anyone.'

Be there, side by side...

His gut twisted, the pain in his chest like a physical burn, his confession riding his tongue— that he loved her, that he always had, that he always would.

But he couldn't tell her, he couldn't vocalise it and tear them both apart. In a month's time, a year, he would be a blip in her past and she'd move on with her newfound career goals and her dream for a family with someone that deserved her and wasn't so messed up.

'I'm not the right man for you.'

'And shouldn't I be the judge of that?'

He released her hand, threw his feet to the floor and gripped the edge of the bed as he hunched forward. 'Ten years ago, I would have said yes, I would have run with what's in my heart, but not now, Catherine. I'm barely happy in my own company. The idea of being surrounded by the masses on your arm, with you so perfect and me like this…and in the face of Fred's loved ones… I can't do it. I can't.'

'I'm not perfect, Alaric. You of all people know I'm not, and yet, you've shown me to love who I am.' He glanced back at her, unable to resist the lull of her words, their importance. 'To look in the mirror and like what I see, without the make-up. To let my hair dry however it may. To eat what it is I want to eat and not obsess about every calorie, every pound of weight. You've shown me that.'

Her voice shook with her sincerity, her cheeks flushed with the passion he'd instilled in her, and for the briefest of moments, he let it in, all of it. How much he loved her, how much it warmed him to know that he'd made a difference for her too. That she wouldn't leave this island the same person she was when she arrived. That she would be happier, more content, healthier.

'And those people, Fred's loved ones,' she whispered, her hand reaching out to rest on his shoulder. 'They will be happy to see you return to the land of the living, I promise you.'

He stared at her, quiet, contemplative.

'You said you were ready to face your guilt, to talk to Cherie, to move on…'

'Yes. I did. And I meant it.' He closed his eyes, his head filling with an anguished Cherie, their child, the graveside and the rain lashing down. He hung his head forward, shutting Catherine out, quashing the hope she was threatening to bring to life. 'But confronting the past and moving on is one thing, having a fairy-tale ending thrust in Cherie's face, in his family's face, is something else entirely.'

'You have a right to find happiness, Alaric, you have a right to—'

'Stop, Catherine, just stop!' The lull of her words, the picture-perfect future she was trying to paint, was crucifying him. 'I can't do it.'

'Can't or won't?'

He didn't answer. He couldn't. Heart pounding in his ears, he thrust up and strode for the bathroom. Hating himself as he did so, but knowing it was the right thing to do. He slammed the shower on, gripped the back of his head and pressed his forehead into the cold stone wall.

She deserved better, she *would* get better, when she was long gone from this place and the web of seduction he had unintentionally created. He got the beauty of the island, the beauty of escapism, and his presence in the midst of it *made* him the right guy for her.

But he wasn't.

And he couldn't fall into the trap of believing that he was because when it all fell apart, he would be the one unable to come back from it.

He'd be the one trying to claw back what he could of his confidence, of his life, with a heart torn in two.

CHAPTER FOURTEEN

SHE'D PUSHED HIM too far, and all because she'd been swept up in the realisation that she loved him. That she loved him and in three days she would be leaving, and this would be over…unless she could convince him otherwise.

She heard the sound of the shower turning on and fought the urge to follow him.

This wasn't part of the plan, her brain warned. Convincing him to return home to his family, yes, and he'd agreed to it. She could finally give Flo the news she'd been waiting for. Her friend would be ecstatic. *She* should be ecstatic too. Her script was almost done. Her escape had given her space to think, time to relax, time to…fall in love.

And that was the problem.

Falling in love hadn't been part of the plan but now that she felt it, truly felt what it was like to be *in* love with someone, she wasn't ready to walk away.

Not without a fight.

She pushed herself out of bed, taking the sheet with her, and froze. She could just make out the corner of a small book jutting out from beneath his pillow. A book she hadn't seen before. She frowned. What would he keep…?

Her eyes flitted to the bathroom and back

again. Tentatively, she leaned over and pulled it out. There were no words, just a plain black cover with a pencil hooked into its spine.

She trailed her fingers over the soft leather. Was it a diary, a notebook, a...*sketchbook*?

Skin abuzz with nerves, with hope—she didn't want to invade his privacy but she had to know— she peeked inside and her stomach came alive. A thousand butterflies desperate to be free as she took in the artist-grade paper, the pencil marks...

Alaric was drawing again; there could be no other explanation for it being under his pillow, in the bed they now shared together.

She opened it fully, her eyes lost in page after page. Various shapes, shading techniques, lines, crosses, smudges...had he been testing himself?

The shapes began to morph into sketches that seemed to be abandoned halfway, of inanimate objects, a glass, a chair...she turned the page again and her hand flew to her mouth.

Oh my God. Was that...?

She dropped onto the bed. Her heart in her throat, her eyes misting over as she saw it for what it was—his first complete picture and it was of *her*.

So obviously her...

She was curled up in the bed sheets on her front, her hair spread out on the pillow, her lips softly parted, her eyes closed. The pencil scratches graduated from light to dark towards the middle, jagged lines, rough, almost wild, but the effect… it was beautiful, impassioned, filled with such feeling.

When had he…?

'You were asleep.'

She jumped, her fingers hovering over the page as her eyes shot to the bathroom doorway. She hadn't heard the shower turn off; she hadn't been aware of anything but the image.

Guilt bloomed in her cheeks, her heart rate wild as she tried to read his expression and failed. How long had he been stood there watching her, a towel around his waist, his body taut with tension?

'You sketched me?' It came out like a whisper.

'It was the only one I didn't bail on…the only one that…' He trailed off, his gaze falling to the drawing as his eyes narrowed. 'I hope you don't mind?'

'*Mind?*' She wanted to laugh and cry at once, her eyes going back to the breathtaking image. 'Are you crazy? It's incredible.'

She heard his footsteps approach, her heart kicking up in her chest.

'Not as incredible as the real thing.'

If her heart leapt any higher, she'd choke on the damn thing…

'Alaric…' Slowly, she turned to look up at him, wet her lips as she took in the fire now blazing in his blue depths. The question was on her lips again. How can he feel so much and still deny it, deny her? 'I'm not ready for this to be over between us.'

He reached out to cup her jaw, caress her cheek. 'We have three more days.'

'Three more days won't be enough.'

'Stay longer. Your script is going well, you can get it finished…' His fingers and his words were gently teasing her, coaxing her under his spell. 'We could even take a trip to the mainland. I can show you the sights I fell in love with, we can…'

But she was already shaking her head, she had to be real. 'I can't, I have press appearances scheduled, a red carpet launch coming up and a new dress to source in all likelihood.'

'Of course,' he murmured, his other hand reaching out, his fingers combing through her hair as he lowered his mouth to hers. 'Reality beckons.'

'This *is* reality, Alaric. Right now.'

'This is too perfect, to be real.'

And she knew he meant it. She could see it in his gaze, his belief that this only existed on his island, safe from the world outside.

She opened her mouth and he trapped her denial with his kiss. A kiss she let him take because it beat succumbing to the pain of leaving, of this being over.

Because this *was* real. This wasn't here today,

gone tomorrow. She'd be feeling it long after she left the island…

Would he? Or would he truly draw a line under it and move on like it hadn't happened?

She couldn't believe it.

She wouldn't.

Three days later, her cases loaded onto Marsel's boat and only Dorothea and Andreas to wave her off, she was forced to accept it had meant more to her than it had to him.

Alaric was as absent as he had been the day she'd arrived.

Looking away from the island as it shrunk in the distance, she rooted in her handbag for her phone. She wanted to update Flo and…she frowned. There was a piece of paper sticking out of her purse, a piece of paper she hadn't put there.

She tugged it out, her fingers trembling as she recognised the artist-grade paper… She unfolded it and the entire world fell away save for the image in her hand. His picture of her.

She gripped the handrail as her knees threatened to buckle, her eyes fixed on the sketch as her vision swam with unshed tears. He'd added a message to her sleeping form.

She dragged in a breath, looked up to the skies that were darkening to a menacing blue, the clouds blowing in thick and fast as she blinked back the tears to enable her to read…

You are you, Catherine.
Only you.
Beautiful inside and out.
Don't ever forget it.
Yours always,
Alaric x

She spun on the spot, gripping the handrail tighter as she stared back at the island, desperate for a glimpse of him. Was he there on the cliff edge, where she thought she'd spied him that first morning?

She leaned closer, her eyes watering against the sea spray and her hair whipping around her face.

'You be careful, Miss Wilde!' Marsel called out. 'The sea's getting choppy with the storm on the rise.'

Slowly, she leaned back in.

'Don't worry, we'll be on land before it's upon us,' he added, misreading her concern.

She gave him a weak smile, her eyes going back to the island, back to him as she willed him to wake up to the possibility of what they could have, if only he'd choose it.

Her. Happiness. And everything in between.

Alaric watched the boat disappear on the horizon, unmoving from his vantage point on the cliff. He hadn't been able to say goodbye, not without cav-

234 BEAUTY AND THE RECLUSIVE MILLIONAIRE

ing and promising her the world, promising her the impossible.

He wasn't sure how long he'd remained there for, only that the rain had started to lash with the wind, waking him from the stupor her absence had induced.

He turned away from the ocean that now rolled with the storm and headed back to the house. The scent of food greeted him as he walked in and his empty stomach made itself known. He hadn't eaten since last night, since his last meal with her...

'Well, it's about time you showed your face.' He looked up to see Dorothea in the kitchen doorway, wiping her hands on her apron. She wasn't smiling. 'Your dinner is ready. You can help yourself. Andreas and I are going to head home, unless there's something more you need.'

'No, that's fine. Thank you, Dorothea.'

He rubbed a hand over his rain-soaked face, forked it through his sodden hair. Weary to the bone, more tired and broken than he'd felt in so long. She stepped aside to let him enter the kitchen, but he could feel her eyes still on him as he took in the food on the centre island.

Souvlaki. His favourite. Only now it reminded him of Catherine and her first night on the island. Had it really only been four weeks ago?

'She loves you, Alaric,' came Dorothea's soft

assurance. 'And you love her. It's as obvious as the love Andreas and I share.'

He heard her, but said nothing...he couldn't. His chest ached too much to speak, his gut writhed and his eyes pricked. And he didn't cry. He never cried, not even after...after...

'Why did you throw it all away?'

His head snapped around, his eyes spearing hers. But all he saw was his pain reflected back at him, his anguish. Outside the storm rallied, thunder rattling the windows, rain pelting at the glass; it was nothing compared to the storm within.

'Come on, love.' Andreas appeared at his wife's side, his hand gentle on her shoulder. 'Leave the man be. We should get going before the storm gets any worse.'

She didn't even blink, her eyes on Alaric as she waited for the answer he just couldn't give. 'You should go... Andreas is right.'

She gave a small shake of her head, disappointment shining in her brown eyes as Andreas gave him a grim smile. 'We'll see you in the morning, Kyrios de Vere.'

He gave the faintest of nods and watched them leave, Dorothea's words churning him up inside. She was right, she was so very right. He'd thrown it all away, Catherine's love, and for what? Because he thought he didn't deserve it, that if Fred couldn't have it, he shouldn't. Christ, if Fred were here now, witnessing his pain, he'd kick his ass for being an idiot. He knew it just as well as he knew he was scared.

Scared of not being able to stack up, because he thought he wasn't worthy, and the world would see it, declare it…a real-life Beauty and the Beast.

But, so what?

What did it matter how the world saw them? Not when he had her love. And she had given it to him, over and over, and he'd what? Done exactly what Dorothea accused him of and thrown it all away.

Hadn't he spent his time convincing her that appearances didn't matter, hadn't she changed, learned from it, from him, and then he'd been a hypocrite. Not only throwing her love away, but his words of wisdom too. Because he was the one who'd let appearances get in the way of what truly mattered.

He hunched forward, his hands gripping his thighs. He felt sick, dizzy, the pain too intense to breathe. He needed to get to her, he needed to say he was sorry, but more than that, he needed to tell her that he loved her too.

He ran out into the storm, stared at the tumultuous heavens above and knew he was trapped. His island, his safe haven, was now his prison. He cursed the sky, let the rain beat down on him, punishing the fool in him.

But he was a fool no more. He knew what he had to do, and a plan was already forming. A plan that would prove he could do it, that he had it in him to not just leave the island but step straight into the limelight…for her.

'I'm coming for you, Catherine.'

And she would be worth every excruciating second under the lens because their love was worth it, and he'd rather face his fears by her side than live a life without her.

CHAPTER FIFTEEN

'HEY, KITTY, YOU READY?'

Luke reached across the back seat, took her hand in his and gave it a gentle squeeze.

She nodded, dragging her eyes from the street, the crowds, the flicker of camera flashes and the excited buzz…

'You sure? You've hardly said a word since we left the hotel.'

'I'm fine, honest.' She brushed down the skirt of her shimmering gold gown and remembered the last time she had worn it. The night she had seduced Alaric…or had he seduced her? A sad smile touched her lips.

She'd been right to think her designer dress wouldn't fit, Dorothea's delicious food and her injury had seen to that, but she looked healthy, and the forgiving cut to the wrap dress that Alaric had taken great pleasure in unravelling had been the perfect choice. Even if it did bring with it such poignant memories. From their first time together, to his insistence that she would look perfect in any dress because all the public would care about was seeing her, not the designer label, not the super-skinny frame, or the heavily made-up face, just her.

And she missed him. Missed him more than

she'd ever known it possible to miss someone. It was as though she wasn't whole, that a part of her had been left behind with him, on his island. Not that he was there. No, she knew he'd gone back to the UK to visit his family, much to their pleasure, and Flo had been so very grateful to her. The emotion in her friend's voice as she'd told her of his visit to see Cherie and her daughter too, that he'd gained what he so desperately felt he needed, approval to live, some form of closure.

It had made Catherine cry when Flo had told her. Happy tears, bittersweet tears, as she acknowledged that he was free of the guilt, and still, he hadn't been able to come to her. And no matter what she did, she couldn't shift the lonely ache inside.

She gave a snort as she took in the crowds outside and recalled Alaric's words to her on the very same…

'For you, it must be worse. Surrounded by people day in, day out, and standing alone…'

Alone and yet surrounded.

'Are you really sure?' Luke pressed. 'I don't think I've ever heard you snort before a red carpet?'

'Sorry.' She tried for a laugh as she touched a hand to his thigh. 'Lost in my thoughts. Thanks for being my date.'

'Any time.'

She smiled and folded her hands in her lap.

Luke had been her rock since her return from Greece. Every press event, every interview, when she lost her trail of thought or lacked the right enthusiasm, he filled the gap.

She couldn't stop herself getting swept away by the memories of the island, of Alaric and the picture he'd drawn, the message he'd written too. It had to mean more. It had to. She'd seen it in his eyes, countless times over—love.

But the more she thought on it, the more she doubted it all. Had it really been there, or had she just projected her own feelings onto him?

It had been over a week, plenty of time for him to have seen Cherie, his family and reach out. Just a call, a message, anything…

The car came to a stop and she took an unsteady breath, unhooked her seat belt as Luke did the same.

'Time to get this show on the road.' His smile was full of encouragement as his door opened and he stepped out into the raised cheers of the crowd. The shouts for him to look this way as he reached back in to offer her his hand. She took it, stepping out beside him, and then it was her name being shouted along with his.

They smiled under the camera flashes, played their part as they were ushered to the barriers for autographs, handshakes, questions, photos…

'Kitty! Kitty! How does it feel to be back with your ex?'

Luke caught her eye as they exchanged a very slight head shake, a subtle roll of the eyes, their smiles never waning.

'Kitty! Luke! This way, what about a shot of the happy couple?'

'Miss Wilde, give us a smile!'

'Catherine!'

She stumbled in her heels. *Alaric?*

Luke caught her elbow, his brown eyes piercing hers. 'You sure you're okay?'

But she was already scanning the crowd. That voice, her name, it had to be him. But he wouldn't...not with all the press, the cameras, the public...

'Catherine!'

She craned her neck trying to see past the tight frontline, squinting against the camera flashes as she reached up on her tiptoes. She didn't care what she looked like, undignified, desperate... it was him, against all the odds, it was him, she just *knew* it.

'Miss Wilde, Mr Walker, we're ready to take you on through.' The procession organiser was there with security, ushering them on from a respectful distance, but she shook her head. She wasn't going anywhere.

'Catherine!'

She spun in the other direction and the crowd parted, realisation sweeping through the masses that something was amiss. Amiss for them, but not for her. And there he was. Straight down the middle, set back from the red rope barrier, his tall and broad frame dominating those around him, his tux cut to perfection, his face, those eyes, those lips…it really was him.

Her breath rushed from her lungs as she swept forward. 'Alaric!'

'Miss Wilde?' The organiser stepped in front of her as Luke cupped her elbow.

'Kitty? What's going on?'

'There's someone I need to go and see.'

He followed her line of sight before coming back to her. 'Is that him?'

She nodded. She'd told Luke everything, she'd had to after she'd stumbled over one too many interviews and he'd started to worry about her health, her state of mind, after all she'd been through. Some of it by his side…

'Will you be okay?'

She nodded, desperation sending her pulse racing. 'Please.'

His eyes narrowed as he took in the desperate flush to her cheeks, the pleading look in her eyes. 'Go. I've got this.'

'Thank you, Luke.' She rushed to give him a peck on the cheek, a delight for the eager cameras, and then she was striding for the barrier.

'Miss Wilde, you can't…' Security tried to intercept her, but she wasn't stopping. Alaric was here, at her movie premiere, where there were cameras, there were journalists, the whole world was watching, and still, he was here.

Security stepped into the crowd, following her lead and creating a safe pathway, and as soon as she was free, she was racing towards him.

'Catherine.' It escaped him in a whisper that brought her up short, her eyes desperately searching his for confirmation of what this grand gesture was. 'You look…incredible.'

Warmth flooded her cheeks, her heart fluttering so wildly she thought it might escape. 'What, in this old thing?'

His smile lifted to one side, camera flashes flickering over him, over her, as the crowd shifted their focus from the red carpet, but he didn't seem to notice. Even as security scurried about keeping them at bay and their shouts built:

'Who's this?'

'Is this a new fella?'

'Can we get a name?'

'Wasn't he in that Avenger movie?'

She laughed at that one, tears choking up her throat.

'I'm sorry I let you go without saying goodbye.' He reached out, his hands gentle on her arms, their warmth permeating her skin, her body, her heart.

'Is that why you're here, to say goodbye?'

He laughed softly. 'No. I'm here to say I'm sorry that I let my fear get in the way of telling you how I felt. That even when I let you go, I should have told you still.'

'Told me what, Alaric?' Hope had turned her voice into a whisper.

'That I love you, Catherine. I love you so very much.'

She wet her lips, tears clouding up her vision. She was going to ruin her make-up, but she didn't care, he loved her. *Truly* loved her.

'Why didn't you?'

'Because regardless of my guilt, I still felt you deserved better, that I could never be pictured beside you and seen as equal. Not by the press, the public...'

'And you think I care about all that?'

'No. That's just it. I don't think you do. But I did.'

'And now?'

'Now I'm here, in front of all these cameras that I feared, in front of the world, telling you that I love you, and if you will have me, I'll spend my life making sure I'm worthy of you.'

She pressed a finger to his lips. 'Don't. Don't say that. You are worthy, you always were, because I love you, Alaric, and I always will.'

She combed her fingers through his hair, pulled him down to her lips and sealed her words with a kiss. The camera flashes and the noise from the crowd escalated with the wild fluttering within her heart, the heat of pleasure swirling through her limbs too, until a honk from a car had Alaric breaking away.

'I think we're causing a scene.'

'Wasn't that your intention?'

'Yes and no, but whoever the celeb is in that new car, they're not going to be impressed that the press are now circling us instead of the red carpet.'

'Then come with me?'

'Now?'

'Yes.'

He looked over her head, at the masses and smiled. 'Okay.'

She smiled with him. 'Even if it means getting your picture taken?'

'I think they already have plenty of those.'

'This one we're posing for…' She led him back to the carpet with the aid of the security team, and the procession organiser approached them, her carefully composed smile taking in their new arrival.

'Do we have space for one more?'

'Unlikely, I'm afraid.'

'It's okay,' Alaric said in her ear. 'I have Flo's ticket.'

'You haven't?' Her eyes shot to his. 'How long has she known? She was drilling me only yesterday about her outfit.'

He grimaced. 'Not long enough. I've pledged many hours of free babysitting in exchange.'

She laughed, so very happy that it almost felt like a dream.

'Kitty! Miss Wilde! Who's your friend? Do we get a name?'

She wrapped her arm around him as he did the same and they turned to face the flashes.

'This is Alaric de Vere…' An excited ripple ran through the crowd as recognition of his name spread and she looked up at him as he looked down at her. He didn't care that they knew who he was, that his scars now faced the camera and they'd capture them in their glare, he only cared for her and it was all in his eyes, his smile. 'The love of my life.'

He leaned closer to her. 'This is going to be the longest film in history, isn't it?'

'What makes you say that?'

'Because there are so many ways in which I want to tell you I love you right now and nearly all of them require us to be alone.'

'Lucky for us I'm wearing the perfect after-party dress.'

He chuckled low in his throat, his mind doing the same journey back in time as her.

'Although…' she murmured, her smile for the crowd, her words for him '…what about a before party?'

He cocked a brow. 'Before?'

'I reckon there's time before the show begins and there's bound to be a quiet corner somewhere…'

His grin turned devilish. 'Are you serious?'

'More than…' She tugged him towards the cinema. 'It's time to live a little.'

'You don't have to tell me twice.'

She was pretty sure she'd told him plenty more times, but she wasn't about to argue the point.

He was here and their life together was truly just beginning.

EPILOGUE

Three years later

'ALARIC, DEAR, THE car is here!'

His mother called up the stairs just as Flo came bustling into the bedroom to help his wife, who was currently enacting some kind of jig in her form-fitting red dress.

'I knew I should have gone for something less... just less...'

Catherine flapped her hands about her, her nerves unusually on show, and he walked up to her, took her hands in his and smiled into her eyes. 'You look spectacular, and Flo has assured me she knows a trick to getting you zipped up.'

She eyed him sceptically as Flo bustled past him and crouched down behind her.

'I sure do, just...give...me...one...*tick*! And *voilà*!' Flo straightened up. 'You're in! This fabric is pure genius.'

'I don't know about genius,' Catherine murmured. 'I'm sure it didn't feel this tight two weeks ago.'

He laughed softly. 'May I remind you that you were only thirty weeks pregnant then? Our little girl has two more weeks on her now.'

She smiled up at him, her blue eyes wide and sparkling. 'True.'

'And the second one always shows more than the first,' Flo added, patting her own tummy that was currently concealing her third.

'You ready?' He smiled down at his radiant wife and gently squeezed her hands.

'I think so.' Her smile wavered and he lifted one of her hands to his lips, kissed it softly. 'You were like this with Max, remember, nine months of hormones and worrying, and out he popped, and you were Kitty Wilde the diva again.'

That earned him a scowl as she withdrew her hands from his and gave him a playful shove. 'Careful, dear husband, or you'll be sleeping in the nursery tonight.'

He chuckled, loving the fire that had crept into her gaze. 'I may need to. I have to be up at the crack of dawn to make sure everything's in place for the charity gala.'

Her smile filled with adoration. 'Have I told you how proud I am of you?'

He reached out and pulled her to him. 'Yes, but you can tell me again if you like. Though the charity venture was your idea.'

'No, my idea was that you joined a support group to talk about what happened, not to finance an entire charity to help others with similar experiences.'

'It was a natural development.'

'And it makes you feel good to know you're helping others. Every time you talk about it, your eyes do that thing.'

'That thing?'

'They sparkle.'

'Sparkle? Are you emasculating me again?'

'Absolutely not. It's *très* sexy…'

He chuckled, his chest rumbling against hers as he bowed his head to kiss her.

'Whoa, whoa, you two—come on! Mum's going to make the driver a cup of tea if we keep him waiting any longer.'

Catherine gave him a quick peck. 'Flo has a point.'

She took his hand and led the way.

His mother was waiting for them at the bottom of the stairs, Max, their two-year-old son, in her arms and Alaric's father just behind. 'Thanks so much for watching the kids tonight.'

'You're very welcome. We could hardly let Flo miss out on her best friend's premiere. Not to mention her and David haven't had a night out in months.'

'Someone say my name?' His brother-in-law appeared in the hallway, bleary-eyed with his hair and tie askew.

'David!' Flo rushed up to him. 'Have you been asleep?!'

'Guilty as charged.' He grimaced as Flo

grasped his tie and wriggled it back into position, attacking his hair next. 'Hey, two kids under three, another on the way, you've got to grab it while you can.'

Catherine laughed. 'You're really selling it.'

'It's a bit late for selling it, my love,' Alaric murmured, kissing Max on the forehead. 'This bun is well and truly cooked. Be good for Nanna and Grampy, okay?'

Max sucked his thumb in response as Nanna gave him a little bob. 'He's always good.'

'As for this one—' he placed his hand on the curve of Catherine's stomach '—not even born yet and she's off to a red carpet premiere.'

Catherine turned to look up at him. 'I'm not sure it's hormones after all, Alaric. This is *my* film, my script brought to life. What if people hate it? What if they don't get it?'

'Shh, my love, you will blow them all away. I promise.'

'You can't—'

He silenced her words with a kiss and earned them a disgusted *'Ew...'* from their two-year-old nephew, who came rushing in and did an about-turn, dashing back out again.

'And I think that's our cue to leave.' Alaric grinned, gesturing for the ladies to go ahead, his brother-in-law too, and then followed, giving his mum a peck to her cheek and his father a hand to the shoulder as he went. 'Thanks again for tonight.'

'You're welcome, son.' His father covered his hand.

'Good luck!' his mother added.

Luck. He didn't need luck. As he watched Catherine step into the car, her cheeks glowing, her stomach blooming with their daughter, he already felt like the luckiest man alive.

* * * * *

If you enjoyed this story,
check out these other great reads from
Rachael Stewart

Surprise Reunion with His Cinderella
Tempted by the Tycoon's Proposal

All available now!